A SCRIBE'S WARNING

HEGEMONY OF HORRORS

Achmed Al Hadid

Melvin E. Bellinger II

"Until we rule together in the new world, every woman must be purified by suffering, to break the spirit of kindness, compassion, and good will, so to emerge the strongest warriors on earth. Let love be ravaged, peace emasculated, and let my lovely horrors eradicate all sense of individuality beyond what is me."

–Gishona, Her Fury, Red Queen of Issacre

TABLE OF CONTENTS

PREFACE

The following passages are an abridged compilation of the many experiences of one Achmed Al Hadid, whilst following the Red Queen, Gishona, as her scribe. *Hegemony of Horrors* encompasses numerous volumes, divulging in acute and excruciating detail, the full scope of Gishona's torment of Patashan's people.

It is important to note that Achmed only included the title as it is now, long after Gishona's fall, while safely tucked away in the security of the Yevana, free from the Red Queen's service. Before then, his volumes' original title was *The Red Queen's Plate*, as approved by Gishona herself. Achmed was initially intent on letting it all go, following his exodus from her service, and wished he could burn every volume. It was not until after a long sabbatical, spanning more than a decade, that Achmed realized the importance of sharing her story, making it known, and letting the world decide what to do.

While what is discussed here might be viewed as utter monstrosity, but for the journey of Achmed, it might not have been discussed at all. It was for him, a matter of rendering it to the world in a way that, despite its vulgar character, could be stomached far better than personally experiencing it, in the event that no one was informed.

Think of it what you will. But do not fear. Remember that you go this journey with one who tread this path before you, having emerged renewed and enlightened.

I'll reserve forewarning for Achmed to issue, himself. His voice speaks from here on.

INTRODUCTION

Hear my representations and understand. Please. I pray you understand.

I walked with the Red Queen, seven years as though more than five times multiplied. In the wastes of a world bleeding, I beheld a great arter (artery) squeezed of all its contents for the fury of one whose hands knew not what to do, but for the power to do anything one could imagine. It was mine to record the folding and flexing of each finger, every vein, every pore, and endure her corruption for the memory of what she loved.

Ours was a world of opulence. The Comempri union afforded us so much. A banquet of trade and innovation. Admittedly the spoils and necessities of old wars. The populace of Patashan numbered in the hundreds of millions. We had jungles, so many jungles, home to millions of animal species. All to be rendered a banquet of devastation.

I walked with a monster who played the might of women, skewered the flesh of men, and made slaves of all. None to be exempt. None to escape, no matter the imitation of kind promises.

Pain was everywhere, manufactured as in the aqueducts which ran through Patashan. Its produce was meant to annihilate all weakness. But to what end? In her, is desire unsatiable, seeming without singular cause. Look again with me. Brave the unthinkable, and unthread truth weaved in thickets of unknown horrors.

Do mind my designations, such as, CX1, CX2, and so forth. These are a numbering system unique to my schema, so that I could find my way whilst collecting my many volumes into this singular text.

When Gishona speaks, I encapsulate her words in this wise, ;; ;; as a more conspicuous identifier.

The language here scribed within is at times an obscure thing, especially where the Red Queen bears her tongue for all to hear. Be not obscured by this. See the meaning of it all, if you so will. Take care. Take time… Time…A game with which we are all familiar. Though, it may not be as familiar with us.

FOREWARNING

To all those who walk this way with me, be warned. The contents herein are wrought with depravity at its most demoralizing. I speak of horrors, as plain as its namesake. I tour the mind of one whose deconstruction of humanity is total. I speak of intimacy, that which we hold sacred, twisted, mangled, turned inside out, and reformed into a raging, rancid nightmare, multiplied many times over. I speak of pain, endless forms of pain, torment, and torture, so beloved by its benefactor, that she made an art of inventing new and increasingly devastating ways of delivering pain upon her intended subjects, even foregoing human capacity to endure it.

In this, there could and can be no remorse. Neither felt by she who invents pain, nor by those she enslaved. Forgiveness, under these conditions, is a hapless, obscure function, only relevant to those who manage to live beyond her. Only relevant enough for the living to shed her pandemonium like the skin of a serpent, so they are not constricted by it, and are able to grow beyond its confines.

If the eating of raw flesh deters you, do not enter here. If the tearing, twisting, skinning, raping, burning, poisoning, and beating of flesh discourages you, haunting your thoughts, then remove from your eyes this haunted text. If the devouring of innocence breaks you, in all its various forms, let this thing go. Leave it to those who are able to process the lessons found herein, and feel no shame in turning away. None should have it a necessary thing to lay sight upon this display.

I love you all... All those who read. All those who find. All those who pierce this bitter mind. I am with you on this sacred journey. The world needs to know, or this may be our reality.

CHAPTER 1

HERE LIES ACHMED

CX1

Here lies Achmed Al Hadid, king of Erushad in the westward Kaius (ky-us) mountains of Patashan, slain by the Red Queen of Issacre, Her Fury (*Her Majesty*), Gishona. In his place was erected Hepatsu, from the body of Achmed, given life by she who takes and gives blood, to forever record all her doings, all that she would have the world remember.

Hepatsu was the name she gave me, the day she elected me to her side. In her early days she showed herself a competent queen, worthy of her father's name and station. So I supported her when she presented herself to the Comempri, of which I was a prime member. And though others stood with me in support of her right to rule, the majority reviled her, insulted by her womanhood, and subsequent audacity to aspire to any throne. Such was the dominion of men, as they believed.

For their repugnance, they were condemned to challenge her in a fight they could not win, and as some would say, had already forfeited by the whims of their beds, and her words adance (dancing or percolating) in their minds. That was the day she came to me as the morning's eye opened, while I was yet in my bed, and told me what I was to do.

;; You will be my scribe. Remain at all times, here my side. Every moment of intimacy, you will see. What I tell you to write, your hands will agree. I will protect you from all harm. You will not need for water or meat. You will never require sleep. And all else, I will satisfy for you. We begin now. Rise with me. ;;

I entertain myself with the idea that I do not yet understand why she chose me, for she did not make it known beyond my prior support of her. But I looked upon myself and understood. I had no family, save distant relations, sixty years under the sun, though to look at me it seemed forty, and as only few knew of me, I had been developing latent sight long ignored in my youth, now unavoidable.

What I see with my eyes, my mind remembers as though always present, and the more I remember, the more I can predict and visualize what is to come. By this, I questioned the relevance of past and future. Are they truly real, or mere constructs of failed memory? For I see so many things as now happening, now being, as I did the moment I beheld Shivana, rather, Queen Gishona, standing at the foot of my bed, with a proud smile of one who had found a confidant among thieves.

I saw her as she always is. I saw what being by her side might afford me, a stream of evolution that would somehow give more than it took from me. I saw in her great madness, a dimness, with a touch of light clashing inside, and I somehow understood, that it would all be well. Somehow, it would be well, or at least I would be.

Without a dot of resistance, I agreed to go with her. I saw that there was no reason to refuse her, that all prior events led to this, a collection of elements harmonizing to attune to this one moment, and I understood that refusal would only result in my torment, enslavement, and someone else doing what I did not. But I had the sight, and she knew it. She could see it in me, in my eyes. That, is what she was most proud of…being remembered.

CHAPTER 2

PAS PARTIS VENERATI

CX2

Pas Partis Venerati. I venerate the past, but in me it is only a participle of an ongoing present moment. This moment, a loving continuum of contrivances, devised by a mind which I can only imagine remembers all things, always. This I imagine because I understand – by what means I am still grasping – that a mind such as mine can only exist if it existed before.

I venerate the past participle, because it must be remembered. The world must be welcomed to the knowledge of the Red Queen, or her blood may again be repeated. Again repeated, for she has happened before. Many times before. She is many times at once. Collective dim ones not knowing where home is, and unable to distinguish any semblance of home from chaotic incarnations.

Am I a continuation of Mal-Jin? the next to inhabit sight, and to be inhabited by it? Was this also the nature of *his* mind? I ask because I feel him nearer to me now than what reverence a Comempri oath can manifest. This is what I thought of Mal-Jin in what many call the past. So, in the past participle I will speak from here on.

CHAPTER 3

FIRST TIME, FIRST MEMORY

On the day the Primaviscera (Prima-viscera) roared with anticipation for the first time, I watched as men were unmade. Men, with whom I once exchanged words and broke bread. I covered my face with a mask so I would not be recognized, and sat amongst the crowd nearest the arena –

So much to write. Where to begin. Truly begin. There are so many memories of the now, or rather, in the past participle. I will begin with what occurs in its own order. Perhaps a path will become clear as I go on. To control the creative is to limit its continuum, choking its ability to continue.

I recall the first time she took me aside to her bed chambers, Queen Gishona. Before this, I hadn't realized how precious I was to her. She cared for me in everything, a man, as if all her reduction of men meant nothing. She fed me, patiently, peacefully, the finest food and drink, the purest water. Lovingly she bathed me, every stroke against my skin a work of art. She sang to herself, to me, beauty in the sound of her voice, smiling as she made me clean, like one who lovingly tends her garden. By her guidance, I wore the finest apparel, as one might expect a king to wear, though I was not king anymore. Graceful were her words to me always, even in anger. She would not have me offended. Why? why this? I wondered. She also dressed my skin with oils to keep it fair. Was I truly so precious? even more than the kings who were promised her affection?

The first time she brought me to her bed, which became every time after, she laid me down gentle, always gentle, always graceful. She overcame me with passions I could not to you with words render, more so than with any other. Why to me? I pondered. Always my sight made sense of things. Images put together according to what was given. She whispered to me, "*What does it feel like?*"

To this I replied, "*It feels like you are everywhere, that every individual part of me is enveloped by you, both singular and multitude.*"

That was how it felt, and so that was what I saw. Gishona multiplied many times over, covering every part of me until all I could see was her. Many as one. That night was the after of the Primaviscera humiliation. She had an ability, what was strange to me at the time, to step through a door and be where she desired. We walked through my door together and arrived at her Primaviscera. And when that was done, we stepped through a door, into her chambers in Issacre.

Why this now? Why this memory first? Perhaps it is because it overshadows all that follows. That is how I saw the Red Queen from then on. One and many. Singular and multitude. Here with me, and everywhere. And such, is precisely how she would have it.

CHAPTER 4

THE RED HALL

I once saw her take a man aside into a great red hall, large enough to hold fifty thousand people exactly, filled with captive onlookers, women and men, all ages, naked, bound hand and foot, seated upright on the floor, their hands behind them, their mouths gagged by a chain around their heads, with an iron ball in their mouths which had human skin sewn over it. Great numbers of the Isscaran surrounded them to watch. The queen dragged her man up to a stepped stage, like the levels of her palace, high enough above everyone else so all could see. He was already in great pain. His body was bruised all over. She had beaten him. The people, wept and quivered with desperate fear. The queen hung the man by chains in the air just above her, with all his limbs outstretched.

I recall so clearly her wretched method. She spoke nothing to anyone for the duration of the act. It might have been as though no one else was present, save her and her victim. At first, she reached her hands into his stomach, right at the navel, and pulled the meat from him, holding it to herself. She ate it with such voracity, licking the bits from her mouth and cheeks, even the blood from her neck with a tongue that expanded in length. The man's screams were sweet to her ears, ushering from her voice, a quiver of her own.

While the blood yet dripped from his wound, she wrapped her arms around his back, dug her face inside him, and drank from his body, somehow drawing more blood to her than was given. Streams of red ran down her neck to her feet. After she drank, she took small bites. Then suddenly, she bore her hands through his wound and tore him asunder, half this way and half that way. She took one half and tore it again, off the chain from which it hung, rubbing her bare body with the exposed inner flesh and squeezing until she was soaked by it.

After consuming what remained, to the last bone, she stood up, basking in her efforts, in the blood, in the waste, and was so satisfied by her deeds that she expelled fluid from her lower regions, further dressing the already soaked stage.

She dragged another man up to her platform and raised a stone slab in the center from out of the floor, in the shape of a bed. She tied the man down, sat upon him, and dug into his skin with her nails, carving his flesh from shoulder to waist, holding at times with eyes closed to hear the rising tones in his screams as though tuning an instrument of music. When she felt they were just right, she broke his legs, twisted his arms, amplifying his pain, and then raped him. As she drove into him with violent repetition, she pressed her palms to his shoulders and crushed them. His wails wrenched tears of fear and anguish from those forced to watch, and filled the Isscaran with pride, until they too shared in the queen's euphoria.

She went on for nearly an hour, forcing out of him all he had to give. And when he could not give, she knew how to make him give more. When it was enough, she ate him as well.

She went through so many men, and did things with their skins, I could not describe, but to say that she played with them as would a child with toys. Always she covered herself with blood. My words pale to the images which saturate my memories. Again, as though no one else were present, she indulged herself, her joys, while all else watched.

Last on this occasion, she took many men, thirty-two in succession, cut a wound with her fingers, and drank them dry of blood to the last man. As they lay dead on the steps of her stage, she walked around to all her prisoners and vomited blood and meat on each of them. No such amounts of any meat or liquid should she have been able to contain.

There was no worthy end for such means. No reason was given, except the obvious play for pleasure. Was this a performance? an artwork for an audience? I knew it. She was proud of what she did. And perhaps, that was the point. She simply wanted to do it. She loved it, and wanted everyone to see. Especially me.

She later took me back to her chambers, still covered in filth, reviewed my writings, and then kissed me. She filled her tub with warm water, removed my clothes and sat me in it. Then she stepped in and mated with me as the blood and flesh washed from her body, poisoning the water with red. While we bathed, the room was cleaned by six handmaids.

Did I want this? There was nothing to want or to not want. The nature of my position was simply to be. I could never feel myself attached to her, but I also had no means of resistance. I felt my body enjoy itself, as though my consciousness a hovering spirit, separate, observing. She would have me enjoy what she did to me, asking if I liked this or that, if it felt good here or there, this way or that way. I could have laughed entertained by the notion that I had a choice, for such an idea was laughable. I could not forget that I was chosen for this. A choice made *for* me. To have refused, would imperil a life in place of my own. Even more laughable, given the peril which would subsume all under her rule. Still, the one life I could spare, was somehow worth it. In all this madness, worth it.

{:} {:} {:} {:} {:}

I write these as they come. My visions of horror. Her story of nothingness made real. Queen Gishona did what she did because it pleased her to do it. But what was the end? I always wondered. Nevertheless, I remember the Red Hall.

CHAPTER 5

THE INNER PYRE

CX5

I had gone before Gishona once into her chambers, following an incident which angered her greatly. It was perhaps the one time she required a moment alone, and indeed it was a moment, for after that amount of time exactly, she entered her chambers to confront me. I thought it untoward that she who would have me witness her every vulnerability, proud of her wrathful ways, would withhold that instant from the eyes she desired to be upon her at all times.

There is a pyre in her, one that existed then and has only increased since. This pyre, this furious fire, she uncovered for me to see. I was sitting on the bed when she prowled to me, lunging her body forward till her face nearly met mine, her hands like tiger's paws, with a stare that threatened to pounce and rend flesh. She demanded I look into her eyes to view the fire within.

;; Look at me. Here within my eyes. There is a pyre in me; do you see it? What does it show you? What do I want to do? ;;

Before I peered within, I felt her fury, the heat of a furnace daring to sear my skin, and a bashing beat as that of many drums, fists against my chest, forcing my body to tremble and my voice to murmur, at first struggling to words form. Then with eyes captivated by the volumes of her pupils, I said:

"I see burning. So many burning. The smell and fumes make horrid the air. Hatred melts the mind before the flames singe flesh. I see you with

them. You burn with them. You bathe in oil and make yourself a fire. As fire burns in you, so too does it burn inside of them. Humanity is but an imitation for you. Its limits are to you, boundless. Whose body have you stolen to play the part? They burn for so long, beyond when death would claim them. They do not die. Their flames light the night, and their screams horrify the night air."

It was when she kissed me after, that I also burned inside, but could not die. I suffered, and did not suffer. I felt all and nothing at once, as though again split apart, calmed by the feeling that all was inherently well with me. She would only have me endure it for a moment, precisely the amount of time she required alone. She licked the tears from my face – sucked the pools from my eyes. Then she bathed me in the rage of her body, drawing me into herself once again. Again, I was not to suffer punishment on her account, no matter the fury burgeoning behind her distilled countenance.

When we were done, and she was satisfied, the Red Queen helped me dress and took me outside to her throne. A large cat cast in gold, which was not present moments ago, sat oddly by the throne on its right. A hole there was in each eye, and its arms were outstretched. The Red Queen ordered fifteen slaves brought to her, all of them naked as she was, awaiting her demands. She gazed at them with flames of fire still flailing behind her eyes, and a dagger tightly grasped by her left hand where it was not, a moment before.

She had tables of wood brought to her throne. She ordered one man be stretched onto a table and tied, his belly exposed to the air. The queen approached him slowly, letting her anger build. She ran her daggerless hand along his belly, up to his chest. Graceful, as if she were touching me. She tasted him with her tongue, driving it along the same path as her hand before. She paused at his lips, kissed them, then opened his mouth and exhaled a black smog inside him. Her gaze, though calm, was vengeance, and the more this man stared into them, attempting to know her intent, the more afraid he felt.

When she was done, the man wanted to cough but could not. He otherwise suffered no disturbance. She ran her hand backward from his chest and stopped just before his indera. Indera for the male parts; oriva for the female.

Then, with a sudden grimace and a swift thrust of her arm, she plunged the dagger into his flesh, half-way deep, and drove it along the same path as her hand, up to his chest, and along each wing of the clavicle. The Isscaran stood by, watching, gaining in hunger as he screamed, and the queen in vengeful satisfaction. She stuck the dagger in his thigh and left it there to free her hands, so she could reach into the opening she scored and pull his belly open. His screams amplified, filling his doomed company with fear. Some of the Isscaran so impassioned by his pain, laid others on tables and forced themselves upon them, using them to satisfy their ardent longings.

After the Red Queen opened her first victim, she poured hot oil into the crevasse, increasing his desperate cries. He begged her to stop. So many confused questions. So many pleas for mercy all mixed and muddled in mangled speech contorted by anguish. But the oil was just the primer. She raised her left hand and from her fingers grew flames, until they engulfed her hand in fire. It was then that she gazed at the man with a devious smile, and he understood what was to come. She laid her hand into the oil from whence she first laid the blade, and set loose the fire. While it roared, she closed the skin and quickly sealed flesh together with her still-burning hand.

The man's screams were no longer his own, erupting into sounds that never a man should utter. The others were torn by the sight, and those unwillingly servicing the Isscaran, broke bones at the hip from the pressure of their captors bearing down harder and faster, urged by overwhelming pleasure as the man's screams intensified.

The Red Queen, herself enthused, roared a dreaded scream of her own. Her rage released. But she had only begun. She ordered the Isscaran to tie all the slaves to tables, whereafter she did to all as she did to the one. And while they were prepared for fire, the first man continued to burn from the inside, his skin boiling, but prolonged. He could suffer, but he could not die. Even as the fire strangely spread through his arms, his thighs, his legs, his hands, his feet, his neck, he could not die, and he could always scream.

The sounds, the sounds, as that of wild animals and creatures unknown to us, tormented and torn apart, or like some demonic beast from the darkest depths of our imaginations, or of hers. This same doom was thrust upon the others. Their cries together, made all of Issacre weep with fear. The golden cat also screamed.

What offended her so? such that so many should suffer seeming endless burning? A child, a boy of ten years, refused to bow and kiss her body in worship of her. This is what ignited the furnace, stirring the coals. The boy was from, of all places, Erushad, my kingdom. He was an exception she made, selecting him as a personal slave amongst the thousands of men she already claimed. A boy of his age would have been sacrificed to be eaten by her. She broke open the golden cat by her throne with her fist, and pulled out the now broken boy, having been forced to watch and listen to everything she did. He could not close his eyes. Her will would not allow. He could not close his ears. His hands were locked inside the cat's arms.

It went on into the night, the burning. More slaves were added to the first, thirty-five in all. The Isscaran were told to hang them where all could see on pikes of iron, three times a man's size and the diameter of a finger's length, on the palace levels and on the ground, where they could continue burning, continue screaming.

The men sat first on their knees where they were to be hung, then the Isscaran opened their mouths and planted the pikes inside, through to the ground. With a mark made for placement, the pike was laid down with the man still impaled and two Isscaran were assigned to a pike.

One grabbed the lower end of the pike by the man's feet while the other grabbed his arms and pulled him to the furthest point just beneath the spear tip. The man's arms were tied crossed behind his back and his wrists bound by a chain which strangled the neck and looped under the arms. The chains were then welded to the pikes by Gishona's hands, as was every man's skin. Finally, the pikes were lifted and planted in place.

The fire by now had spread from within to without, consuming the skin and all else. They would eventually die, but the Red Queen forced it to take time, where nature would have ended their suffering long before. And she, she watched. A captive audience, standing with lax posture, motionless – an idle child seduced by starlight. When she did move, it was to lay on the ground while she watched. And I was there with her.

I at once stood, but then sat upright beside her, hiding the ache of my soul. She came up behind me then and again sat, her arms over my shoulders, clasping my chest, her legs wrapped around mine, and her head against my neck. I felt her breath on my skin. She kissed me softly and hummed a sweet melody. Were we meant to be watching a sunset? as lovers might? Is that what she thought of this? What manner of woman was this? I thought.

And the boy. She raped the boy before she stared at the fire, before she sat with me. She raped him for more than an hour, then set him ablaze much the way she did the burning men. She held his body before her eyes while fire enveloped him from the inside, with a hard grimace scorching her face. She opened her mouth as her rage escalated, releasing tears from her eyes and fire from her pores which clothed her body. With him, she burned, and as he wailed, the fiery queen ate him one bite at a time, until all she held in her hands was his hair and kidneys which she preserved against the flames. With these leftovers, she fashioned a necklace and wore it proudly.

After we sat for a time, the Isscaran gathered around to watch with us. Then the queen had another idea. She was moved, you see, inspired to dance. She began slow, steady, graceful. She felt her body as though her own lover, her eyes closed, surrendering to complete satisfaction with her works. The Isscaran were equally inspired. They brought drums for some to play and a careful beat broke through the torrent bellows of flame. They matched the movements of the queen, gaining in speed and volume until a wild rhythm took shape. The Isscaran joined in the dance, bare bodies flailing, flinging in the night air, myself in the middle of a rapid circle, watching all things.

Eventually my stillness was noticed. They kept glancing at me, smiling, drawing closer. In their enchantment, they looked to the queen and she, knowing their intent, said graciously, *"Be gentle."* They understood how important I was to her, and why. I knew what was coming. I understood what she allowed. And they did. They patiently removed my clothes and neatly set them aside. Then they overcame me and took turns, fulfilling themselves at my expense. I was again beside myself, not knowing what to feel, despite feeling so much. They soon overwhelmed me, crawling about body like ants, though larger than their catch. I became the meal they entertained but did not eat. Wild and forceful it was, but still gentle.

I saw the queen when visible, once limbs and fleshy foliage cleared my view. She was smiling. Her eyes were large and dazzling. She stuck her tongue out at me for a tease and licked her lips for a taunt. They finished me by emptying their fluids onto my body, and showering upon my head, then they took turns rubbing my face against themselves where their fluids were still dripping. I could not show any displeasure. The queen giggled at the sight, before she too did the same. But when it was done, she took me back to the palace and things went as they always did. I recorded what I saw, she bathed me, we bathed together, and then she mated with me.

So much to think on had I that night. So much. I wondered at the "why?" of my circumstances. Why so many pleasures unsolicited? Why have me enjoy it? Why allow others like her to enjoy me? Questions were never truly questions, for as soon as I asked, the answers met my queries in transit, as though two people passing by in opposite directions, exchanging a letter at the precise instant they meet without ever stopping, and continuing on their opposite paths.

As for the answers, this was my torment, for all that my queen could give to a man so precious to her. There was no good that could come of refusing. No refuge for sanctity of mind to be found in saying, no. I had no say. I was hers to use as was any other man beneath her. The only token of goodness I had was how she cared for me, saving me from a prolonged life of horrors menstruated by pain. Beyond this, was her imitation of loving affection, all of which I was to feel, knowing I could not experience the affection of one who loved me, just as she would have it.

At times, I did rest, laying back in bed beside her, allowing my eyes to close and enter a meditative state so that my mind could maintain itself, all the while fully aware of my surroundings. Perhaps more aware than otherwise. She enjoyed taking advantage of me then, making me feel things, attempting to insert herself into my thoughts and imbue my visions with her. She would not stop until she heard my whimpers.

In my wake state I pondered my condition long and thorough, putting pieces together, members of a great portrait congealing, crafting visions of things to come. I wept for the boy inside myself. Then I laughed at the bewildering thought that another man might not have been able to maintain his sanity in all this, or would believe the queen actually loved him. Was it strange that I was glad it was me instead of another? Again, I understood that all was well with me. I felt it all over. A great warming light. And as it pierced the torment due me, that which was cloaked by the image of loving affection, I saw that it might unweave her torment also, and just in time. For now, a pyre stirred within me as well.

CHAPTER 6

THE FUMES WE BREATHE

The fires of the burning men ushered an unnatural black smog into the sky. It spread throughout the kingdom, carrying with it a putrid, disturbing odor which sickened many. Citizens complained of the sensation of burning from the inside, though much less severe, and of the body's unwillingness to digest because of the horrible smell smothering their senses. When was it all? The pyre and its subsequence were a month after the complete occupation of Patashan. The Primahorica had begun in other kingdoms. This was when the Red Queen Gishona reveled in her apparent victory.

I wrote that people complained, but only to themselves and each other. With the Primahorica dominating all things, there was no rushing to the feet of the queen to tell of troubles that she might show mercy and heroism. A little more pain was pluum a' treviin (plume-a-tre-veen: par for the course). And citizens? What were citizens in Issacre? All were slaves or potential Isscaran. Anyone left to lead the common life, did so to ensure that cities were maintained, sanitized, and that food was farmed and harvested. Even that was a means of keeping those not sustained by raw flesh healthy for the conception and continuation of human subjects, mostly to make for more meager slaves. The queen was *improving*, as she saw it, the meaning of human, and more importantly, the meaning of woman. Men needed to be as healthy as possible so she could tear it all away, through torture, hard labor, or by feeding them to new Isscaran recruits.

Money was collected only as tokens of conquest. There was no commerce anymore, and there would never exist any need for it again in Gishona's territory. Primahorica was to be the transforming mission that would rewrite the world. It would not have been many years from then that the queen would trouble the seas in search of what lay beyond Patashan, provided her reign lasted that long.

In a world successfully conquered by the Red Queen, I suspect that some nations would be kept intact, so there could still be enough difference between the governed and those who govern. Surely the queen and the Isscaran would need to be entertained by the common peoples, whether to spread fear, torment, rape, make toys of them or slaves, eat them, and whatever else they would think to do.

What of the other kingdoms during this time? Those not already consumed by the Primahorica, lived as prisoners awaiting its imminence, ever under the eyes and ire of the Isscaran. They were swiftly dissected into separate groups in preparation for their time, whensoever it came. Women were separated from their families and forced to live in designated districts. Men were made to care for their children so they would not die.

Isscaran took the place of some of their wives, forcing men into sexual givings every night or whenever else they desired, and abusing the children in any way they chose. The Isscaran never wore clothes. They had no need, like their queen. They were neither scorched by the sun nor stricken by cold. They were beyond sickness of all kinds. And they loved for their bodies to be feared and admired by people of all ages. Going into the children's beds was a favorite of theirs – one they most enjoyed. Some of them were mothers once, and would be horrified by what they did then. I was.

The irony, is that it is having to endure the sight of such abuses which begins the process of the Isscaran way for mothers of men. To have the mind torn apart by unimaginable horrors is how the queen breaks them. The first step of Primahorica. But the first women, they had a choice. Downtrodden by society, the queen sought them out to give them reason to rise against their oppression. In so doing, whether they loved and were loved of their families or not, they chose to slay and burn them within their houses, setting ablaze the places they called home to rein in the new way, helmed by Her Fury. Were they fortunate, to have avoided torture and torment – forced change? Or were they given the choice because they were tormented already? Dead wood simply in need of the right spark. Some of the original question now, pondering the why of the queen's changed mind. But questions of this kind wither as the leaves of Pelshar's pale, preparing the way for Asher's cold.

The burning within, once benign, did eventually accrue to its full potential. What was an imitation of the scorching of flesh from inside, soon felt to those afflicted as though they were truly on fire beneath their skin. Never outside, and as always, they could not die. It lasted days before subsiding, forever days.

The crying, the weeping, the wailing aloud, the old, the young, pierced my façade of fortitude, such that I could not hold fast, even in the presence of the Red Queen. Yet, as I wept in her presence, my head in my hand, I felt gentle hands wash over me from behind, arms gathering around mine, breasts pressing against my back, her breath on my neck, and a tender kiss…Hah…an imitation. She sang to me a hum, rocking me in her arms to a gentle sway. It was not to say, "Be comforted." It was not to ease the burden of sorrows within me. It was to say, "This is how it is meant to be." *She*, meant it to be this way.

And the boy, the still-burning boy. His name, Hapanin (Hah-pa-neen). I felt him, still. I knew him more in death than in life. An imitation. His fumes were still fresh in my nostrils, but they were not of scorched remains. They smelled sweet, as one made free. An imitation…How? Was it his kidneys, his hair, harnessed round her neck? But then, as is the nature of questions with me, I understood and let it be. She need not know how power strays from her.

Beyond the sorrows filling our lungs, I smelled something else on the air, a graceful quiet, an uncanny breeze. I felt it in the sun's light. It spoke to me. It said, *"Air of quiet, stillness makes whole, descend and desist. What comes after, waters to stream, what they bring with them, more than what seems. Prepare now the drylands for drinking and fill. The deluge emerging for all those who will."*

Why do such messages come to us in code? Because they are of a language absent the limits of words. We confine all to what we know and what we can describe in verbis (verbiage). So what comes to us free of limit, can only be articulated to us in limited tones that we can understand, for we otherwise refuse to listen beyond our own understanding. Though, some of us are more willing to this than others. As such, even I must render to you what you can understand, for my mind is at all times open to the limitless. I heard the full tones on the air, clearer than words convey, as it is with the constant feeling that all is well with me, which needs no reason for being that I could bottle and seal. It is ever flowing in its natural state.

Why did *I* receive this message? I received it because Gishona would not. She was oblivious to any such sounds, cut off by her own will. It was truly intended for all, but especially her. The need to control all things does dull the senses to subtlety, leaving subtlety to the subtle. I inherited her next of kin, because I was the closest she had to family. Nevertheless, an imitation, but an imitation would have to do for the time.

Something was set to arrive. The air was its herald, the streams before the deluge in a dryland. It would have been appropriate for me to relay this message to the queen, but of course, what message? She wouldn't understand what it means.

CHAPTER 7

DIABOLIC

CX7

Could you imagine the pain? the torturous pain? the pain of being forced to brutalize your son, your father, your brother, so that the children might live? Thousands upon thousands of men, young and old, were made to fight. It was the greatest act of sacrifice and humiliation bestowed upon the male population.

They did not comply in the beginning. They resisted, naturally. But the Red Queen was quick to show the futility of their resistance. She threatened the devastation of the young women, should the men disagree, and she further exemplified her determination by eating insubordinates alive, which she encouraged her soldiers to do.

The men had already born witness to the strength of the Isscaran, even as they pulled some men aside and beat them bare-fisted. They knew they could not challenge them, not even united. The Isscaran outnumbered them as well – three to one. And there was no threat that the Red Queen did not satisfy. Her words were as much deeds as the deeds decreed by them.

Some, lost all sense of pride and ran to the foot of the steps with raised hands, surrendering their bodies, pleading that they be spared shame and torment. Futile. The queen found this amusing and had them rounded up to be brought to the first level of the palace. There, she and her Isscaran skinned them alive for all to witness, then laid them on the floor and emptied bodily waste onto their exposed flesh. The queen bent herself over, laughing aloud at their screams.

No way out. All there was left, was survival. Maybe those who remained after all trials were fulfilled could somehow repay this insurmountable debt and carry on where those before them could not. Maybe their daughters would have something to live for after all, if they could live long enough.

This too was futile. The cruelty of the Red Queen was such that the daughters of men would be torn apart to become Isscaran regardless of anything that men did or did not do. It was either do as the Red Queen demanded, or be food. So they did. They fought one another.

Blood and flesh were rent from living souls. Tears and grief did worse. Many were petrified by their deeds and either killed mercifully, or at the edge of punitive violence. Some who could not contain their grief, exhausted it at the behest of forced rage to supplement what courage they lacked, driving themselves to believe they must persist, or their young women would perish. There were those who feigned courage in the hope of maintaining their claim to manhood. This was equally futile, causing them to exhaust themselves more quickly.

The greatest offense of all, maybe, was that this first trial emancipated the true monsters among them, men who would otherwise be hidden in the brush of humanity, awaiting their finest opportunity to commit devastation. Some, had come to realize they could be monsters, and enjoy it.

There was one man whom, in the beginning, the queen selected to sit at the foot of her throne. There was a division of all men made to fight at the start. Two even groups positioned opposite one another. But there was one more, and so this man was chosen by Her Fury to be chained at the wrists, upper arms, and ankles, with a length of approximately three lexims loose (three feet), so she could move him around when she wanted. He was the largest and strongest male of all, not the tallest though very tall, but having the most muscular mass, hidden by a hulking distribution of body fat. A well-proportioned wall of a man. A fitting example of premier manhood, and perfect for what would come next.

As the fighting hemorrhaged, the Red Queen ran her fingers along his body, squeezing and pinching his skin as she relished in how thick and firm he was, yet soft and malleable. And when the brawling blossomed in blood, she grew so aroused by it that she bit into his face, the cheeks, delighting in the taste, as well as his painful cries. This would of course continue. As precarious as the queen could be with her food, she did have a special purpose for this one.

Eventually, most men grew tired of the fight, aching of physical strain and demoralization. So many, utterly horrified by what they did. At this point, the queen stopped everything. There were over five hundred thousand remaining. After only a moment, she spoke boldly, projecting her voice over the masses, which echoed in such a way that all could hear with precision, and ordered the men to fight until one of any two opposed could not fight any longer. She forbade killing for this round. Though if some died, it was nevertheless pluum a' treviin.

Another brave man, turned to cowardice, stepped out from the masses and boldly approached Her Fury, complaining and crying in so many words that he couldn't do it anymore and had given up. He was a middle-weight, middle-aged man with no family, who lost the will to continue.

The Red Queen was again amused by this, expressed in the widening of her eyes like a startled cat, and a playfully wide grin. She leapt from her throne as he drew near, pounced on him, and dragged him up to her platform where, before her selected prisoner, she laid the man down on his back and ate chunks of him, bite for bite, until after mere moments, he was half his weight. She was careful to avoid vital organs so that he would remain alive, though she would still keep him alive, even if death could not be avoided by natural means. She then hung him from one of her standing braziers so all could see.

Shortly after this, the fighting continued, leaving just over a hundred thousand still standing, while the rest could barely move. Finally, the queen allowed them a few moments rest. But that was far from the end. It was not long before she ordered them to bring those beaten to her as sacrifices, forcing them to risk injuring themselves further on the steps of her palace, a relative mountain to their tired, feeble legs. Stumbling on the way up was common, and some tumbled back down to their deaths, at times taking others with them.

At the top, the Isscaran waited to receive and organize the queen's sacrifices at each level of the palace by taking the side stairways back down. The Isscaran could easily have carried the sacrifices themselves, which for them would have been the equivalent of carrying small tree branches that one might expect a child to play with. But of course, this torturous errand was by design.

The men had to bring their fallen opponents to the top, where along the way, each would see those who first surrendered, and then at the top, what remained of the largest man, now two thirds less than himself, missing his right arm, and struggling to breathe. Every man had to realize that he amounted to no better than waste or food. The queen's palace grounds were anointed with blood when it was done, stained by red bodies and open wounds. These, sacrifices, were simply piled on top of one another, whether dead or alive. No more than heaps of meat for meal. There were so many thousands that some were taken inside.

From this time, now hours later, while the sun was still hot above, until morning, the victors of the first trial were allowed respite. Respite is such an inadequate inverse of the truth. They could not go home to comfortable lodgings, or even to those finest within the palace. They were welcome to the hard, blood-soaked ground of the palace plaza where they fought. And though tired enough to slip into seamless slumber, their senses were eviscerated by the cries of both men and children, as the queen and her Isscaran feasted on their sacrifices all the remaining day and night, immersing them in maddening horrors whilst the daughters of men watched. Sanity was sadly, and easily, lost. Even those intended to rest, wept and wailed with the dying, joining in the choir of death. Should a child lose sanity so young? Should anyone?

And where was I in all this? Right where I always was, ever the observant specter, as the stoic, standing lion of stone, watching placid, bearing all my sorrows inside, even all the sorrows of Issacre. As I listened and observed all things, I too was observed by the ardent eyes of predators, looking back at me as they raised their heads to glance, live meat hanging from their mouths, pausing to study my undeterred stillness. Was I the prize they could not have? Did they wonder what I tasted like? Or were they more concerned with what I thought? Such a unique perspective mine must have been to them. The only man who could see all without breaking, my sorrows tempered always by that uncanny feeling that all was well with me.

Of course, the queen's eyes were foremost. I understood her fascination, that she could look upon me with any intent and still I remained as I always did. I realized all the more, at each point of turning, that despite these seeming insurmountable horrors, I belonged here. Not that this manner of mess was ideal for me. But I understood that no matter the mess, I would thrive. That nothing could withhold life from me. And that, more than all else, this age of horror was to be short-lived, swift to pass, and I was to move swiftly and joyfully beyond it. I could offer an alternative state of events, but such is a pointless spat of words and meaning. That which was true for me then, was true before the horrors came to be. I would always live. I must live. The world needs to know.

This was not the end of their great humiliation. Consummation was the final act of submission to Her Fury. With the men far too traumatized and weary to rise to their feet, flocks of Isscaran descended from the palace and dragged or carried their subjects, each to his own house. The queen ordered that every man remaining was to be given in intimacy to her leading women, and enjoy, or at the very least, allow whatever the Isscaran intended to do.

The Isscaran were forbidden to harm them, much less eat them, except they showed disloyalty, at which point, anything could happen. Passive catatonia was considered loyal enough, as it offered no threat of resistance. To allow the Isscaran to have their way, was to pass the final test. Every spouse of a man alive for this trial was brought in to watch the affair as part of their breaking process.

This portion was not a matter of violent rape, but the imitation of love. The Isscaran were mostly gentle and took their time, bathing their subjected in the experience. The torment was apparent. The Isscaran hated them, and the men were to fear and enjoy each moment, rejecting the temptation to reject their captors. They had to endure every subtle touch, the feeling of breath grazing the skin, the sounds of foreign tones streaming throughout their flesh, and the clutching, dominant passions of those who were not their lovers. The Isscaran often began by licking the dirt and blood from their bodies, even the wounds clean. All else went however it could go, and their lovers watched in agony.

Some of the monsters among men, did enjoy what they received, though horrified by not having any control over their circumstances. The Isscaran had mercy on these, valuing their will to dominate and to violence, permitting that they fight back before subduing them. The Isscaran enjoyed the struggle, albeit meager. They enjoyed letting their captives try to overpower them, basking with ardent eyes in the steady decline, the will of men so bent on control withering into frustration, and from frustration to sorrow.

The Isscaran often teased and taunted. Everything they tried, every motion, push and pull was swiftly turned against them, until they realized they could never have gained the advantage. They were as ants, believing themselves lions, then forced to bear the reality that they are indeed ants, and nothing more.

At the end of the struggle, the Isscaran congratulated their tenacity. They were tied down, stretched out, completely immobilized, and gagged – all control lifted from their being. Then continued the feast of false love, their bodies a banquet of pleasure in which they could not participate. It was a process many times repeated until these men were exhausted. When it was done, the Isscaran stood over their heads so they could look up at those who conquered the conquerors, and anointed them with wet and wasteful streams, promising that to endure this complete loss of control would earn them the greatest favor with the queen. Their monstrosity was of great value to her.

For those captives whose wives stood watch, a bitter bite lie in wait to bore into the flesh. There were usually three or more Isscaran to a man given in marriage, and they loved to gaze proudly, tauntingly at the women looking on as they licked the blood of battle from their husbands' bodies, savoring horrified reactions to every stage of the mating process. To bear this pain in silence was best if the women wanted their husbands to survive their final test. Horror was amplified if the men were seen to enjoy the occasion as well.

For certain women, wives of insubordinate men, this proved a moment of initiation. If the Isscaran saw potential in a woman, they would have her kill her husband and start down the path of monstrosity. But the twist and grind of teeth was found in this. For the women to rebel whilst their men submitted to their captors, the men were ordered to take up blade and carve the skin of their wives to prove their loyalty. Each score with a blade was to be long and careful.

If, however, both husband and wife were complicit in protest, the women were held naked above their husbands and disemboweled, punishing men with the waste of their beloved, then to have fresh blood and entrails eaten off their bodies by their captors while they lay stricken with devastation. They were already exhausted, broken, their minds mangled by horrification, then to witness this. Though many were tortured and devoured for their disloyalty, some men were left alive for months after, to ruminate on their condition and drown in endless loss.

Theiander, my dear Theiander, if only you could have come sooner. The weight of this burden devastates all comprehension for the floods of pain inbound from an ocean whose depths we cannot take in. Why so long? seven years, each a lifetime of perils as the rushing of storming sands in ceaseless waves. Seven years older, and yet, I am the same, a product of both Gishona's unwillingness to see me grow old and the life energy within, gaining in unceasing expansion. That my wellness could make well the undone. Why am I the only benefactor? Is there not another? Still, I live on, as I must. The world needs to know.

The Red Queen had her own process, having gathered a gallery of enslaved men to endure being overpowered by her without the threat of death or torture. She preferred to find things, little things that were to them uncomfortable or bothersome, and torment them with it, as they knew they could do nothing to stop it.

I wondered why the leisurely approach, given her love of monstrous violence, but she did love to remind men of how powerless they were, whether in great extravagant displays of might, or in the small things. She wanted them to know that no measure of control could be withheld from her.

Despite there being rules to this last trial, the Isscaran could do as they pleased, and they knew it. It was only their loyalty and love for their queen which held them taut. But all they needed was to have their way and claim a man's insubordination when it was done. In the end, those who perished, perished, and those who lived, lived. Though, perhaps death would have been best.

Within a month after the trials of men, to honor the sundering of Issen males, queen Gishona dispatched contingents of Isscaran throughout the continent, to empty every settlement not under the jurisdiction of a kingdom, of their male population. Because of their enhanced physique, the Isscaran were able to run at full speed without pause, condensing a journey worth of weeks to a few hours. Once men and boys were apprehended, they were made to walk that week's long journey back to Issacre.

Upon their arrival, the male subjects were stripped of all affects at the base of the palace and imbued with the queen's energy, so they would not die. Afterward, they were skinned alive and marched inside the palace. Over the next few days, the queen sat on her throne, waving her hand over the palace as though a spirited artist, causing slits to open up in its walls and moats to extend from them to trail the edges of the plaza. Out of the walls came streams of water, and after a few days more, blood. Two parts blood; one part water, flowing throughout and around the palace grounds.

To better address the transport of great masses, the queen later built fifty large carriages of iron, able to carry one hundred passengers, having eight crude iron wheels on either side, with many spikes and jagged grooves for traversing harsh terrain. Rather than rely on beasts of burden, the Isscaran themselves pulled them, six to a carriage, by chains and harnesses which functioned as a type of armor they could wear, to make full use of their strength.

CHAPTER 8

THE GLUTTON

CX8

Shall I tell you about the arrival of Theiander? Oh, no. It has no place here. Somewhere else in the writing. For now, I must speak of the glutton. The Great Glutton, who in a swift and all-consuming cloud of deep regression to a less than despotic state, stowed herself away in her red hall and ordered the bodies of men to be brought to her in large numbers, alive as always.

This was one year after the Battle of Balashah, or massacre, if you prefer. Men were brought to her from every region of Patashan. The journey was long, costing of days, which meant that the Isscaran had plenty of time to rape them along the way. Time which they took full advantage of. They subjected them to whatever else they could use them for and still deliver intact. Still, a relative peace offering compared to what they were bound to endure.

Come the end of their journey, the Red Queen had them thrown into piles around the room, tied to their bindings. By that time, the queen's center platform was dressed with gold finery about its rim, and large gold chalices, seven, stood on its surface. While living bodies filled the hall, the queen stood mid-platform, staring proudly as though eyeing her fresh catch after a hunt. I wonder if wild predators are so proud.

What became of the men of Patashan once the doors closed? Blood. Endless blood. The Red Queen began by imbuing them with her energy so they would not die, and then tore them apart in any way she could think of, carefully draining them of blood. She drew it out by the tips of her fingers, focusing their flow into canals surrounding her platform. Not a drop was left inside a drained body. They filled the walls, you see, to make for her to shower herself with red dew, to bathe in excess.

It rained from the ceiling, it poured from streaming falls, drenching her body, and into her favorite chalice. Within a red, soaked, slippery, sticky bog, she tortured as a child at play, tearing and stretching, pulling and prying apart, licking and sucking and biting, branding with fiery hands, slicing with claws, crushing and beating, inserting and withdrawing – all manner of whatever came to mind.

Ever the artist, she stretched and twisted piles of still-living men about one another, molding them around bones and skulls, searing flesh together until they formed a bed of bodies fit for a king. She went on showering herself with blood, grinding flesh and entrails to watery paste to be consumed as though soup. She made a kitchen where she could perfect the craft.

The queen was only to be bothered if absolutely necessary. The Isscaran could otherwise rule as they chose in her stead. And the longer she stayed away, the more foolish she deformed. She became lazy and lax, lying on her bed, drinking blood all the hours, silly, a drunken, sleeping predator, defecating where she lay, regurgitating blood only to slurp it up again. She sometimes dropped her chalice, replacing it with an open skull until she next decided to pick it up again. Blood dripped from every part of her. She of course pleased herself when she felt inclined, and had a ready stem of male flesh to awaken at any moment – whatever part she desired to use.

When at once she did fully animate, inspired, she took to gathering small bones and fashioned for herself a dress of bones, parading around the red swamp in pools of sewage as though a crowd watched in awe. Awe did fill the room, as the now common sounds of screaming, crying, and anguish never ended. The smell was not for anyone's sanity to bear. But I did, in my own corner of the chaos where I could see all things, as always.

This was the most disturbing sight for me, of all that I had seen of her. It was frightening to see her this way – pure parasitic – with no other purpose than to consume, regurgitate, and consume again, as though herself a slave to her own will, nevertheless fully and happily compliant. I felt endangered for the first time – that she could turn on me. She could always turn on me, but I was selected for a purpose, one she was too proud to forfeit, so long as I maintained my station. Yet here, in this state of mind, it seemed she could barely tell one man apart from the other, whether he lived or was dead.

At once, I looked away in thought, and when I again turned to see her, there she was before me, blood dripping from her lips, her whole body, eyes pensive, as a beast lost in hunger, deciding when to strike at its prey. Did she recognize me? She waited, her body wavering in a drunken wobble. It was not until my fear reached its peak that a wide grin spread across her face, and her eyes widened at me. She found it within herself to play at my expense, even in her drunken state. Or was it that I turned away and she again sought to arrest my focus? It was then, as she walked back to her bed, that I realized the smell was its most repulsive when she was near.

Existence in that hall eroded the memory of time. There was a stillness about that place in its mutilated condition. The air did not flow, giving way to the must and mire suffocating all uninhabited space. To breathe was to open the door to an invisible smog of stink, hot, hazy moisture, and the collection of deathly fumes emitted from every heap of flesh contained within.

My lips remained sealed, my energies concentrated on filtering the smog so that I might welcome the freed air. I did not know that I could do this. It was a subconscious act of preservation, perhaps a gift from whatever massive mind extends beyond my own, here in this experience.

I at times found there to be no distinction between this greater thing, and myself, as though a me not bound to mortality, yet still me. It otherwise seemed like a dark dream, a moment and an eternity at once – indistinguishable – and so, out of time.

One moment I was a dreamer, adrift in a red darkness; the next, I was alive with restored sense of place and self. Queen Gishona rose up and stepped onto the blood-soaked floor in such a displaced waking state, as if the sun's light on her eyes, that it seemed she had been somewhere else all the while and another in her stead. She put on her gown of bones and looked around as though unaware of all she had done – unaware of me. For an instant, I was a stranger to her eyes, staring into all my being to recall my relevance to recent memory. In another instant, she snapped to normalcy and carried me across her arms, saying, *"Come, my bejeweled Hepatsu. I have had my fill here."*

Approaching the doors, opening without hands before us, she spoke in cryptic tones, these words: *"Let this well of wailing spread. Let the eater feast. Let the taker consume. Let the maker carve my caverns deep, and expand the anguished until their suffering satisfies."*

I heard and felt rumbling as the doors closed behind us. The earth moved. She bathed me in her palace as always, and herself as well, expressing the wet cleanness of her body to me whilst she washed – yet another performance. The gown of bones she had prior hung on the wall. When she took me to bed was when my scribing began, and she watched me with a scandalous adoration until it was done. I note that with each entry into her sacred pages, the need to write evaporated a little more, until I had only to look at the pages for memory to become words.

Upon completion of the task, she grinned a wider grin than customary. Something different then. She laid me down in my nakedness and came over me, looking first into my eyes and then to her right, at the door. Another Gishona stepped in and joined her on the bed, then another, then fifty more, all gathering around me, beneath me and upon me. A cocoon of Gishonas filling every gap until all I could see was her. They held my head, my limbs, every part of my body. For an instant, I felt fear, thinking I did not know what this was. But fear bowed respectfully to memory, ushering in the vision of our first encounter here, and my words, *"It feels like you are everywhere, that every individual part of me is enveloped by you, both singular and multitude,"* now made physical.

The things that they – that she – did to me, I did not have words for, or reason for why she wanted me to feel so much, beyond her enjoyment of infecting my memory with herself. Did she want to be inside of me? to steal *my* body as well?

I escaped, that night. This time, not as if. Enough of me departed my flesh to flee the overwhelming swarm of feeling. She saw me They tried to catch me on the way out, as I lifted into the air. When that part of me was gone, they intensified the fest of feeling, attempting to reach my departed self by other means. The sounds they made were as one so desperately hungry, digging her face into a bowl of delicious food, and passionately enjoying every bite. I still felt all they did, yet nevertheless free. It went on for hours. My body screamed. My body screamed. I don't know why, but it did, and the answers are left to the obscurity in which they could be found. I suppose our occasion with the Isscaran was a rehearsal for this.

In an instant, it was done. In an instant, I returned. In an instant, they were gone, but she was still there. I was shivering, trembling, as the waning vibrance of the mighty gong, long after it is beaten. I was curled as one who is cold, still shielding myself from an experience now empty. She pried me open again, and with tenderness, kissed my body. I winced each time, still so fragile. This was not an apology, neither a truce. It was a finishing touch. And when finished, she left me.

The irony. It was then that I felt I needed the warmth of a lover to hold me, and undo the rape of the imitation. I felt so very alone, so torn and tattered, so naked – the skin ripped from my flesh as if. Then…then, I understood. She had grown tired of my well-being – of my connection to whatever guarded my soul, and just once at least, she wanted to control that connection, to own me that much more. Nevertheless, as always, all was well with me, and all good things returned, as I let go her illusion of power.

The glutton, is always immersed in the illusion, so afraid to lose what it has, that it consumes all it gains, until it gains the loss it sought to lose.

CHAPTER 9

TROPHIES

CX9

There is another red room, disease infested, blood and fungal growths smothering the walls, where from their faces, and from the ceiling, hang a seeming endless gallery of entrails. Tied and twisted together, loom the cords of our inner parts, like strings dangled, or grand arrays of fine drapes clothing bed chambers. They are everywhere.

The hall itself reaches a height which cannot be determined as it hides above red mist, and it is so long a tunnel that the end seems naught. It is lit beyond the aid of perceivable source, yet glows as if by fire, and the light is evenly spread to create an unseemly ambiance affecting the entire corridor.

Mingled with entrails of all forms, of every part of us, are the loins of women and men alike, sometimes whole, sometimes stripped of skin, constantly bleeding beyond what nature allows.

Infused with the blood and fungal growths, are heads, frozen in terror, skin torn or cut, stretched, bludgeoned, or mixed with bones, intestines, and anything else. There is a section devoted to male skins, processed as though leather, stretched and hung for display like drapery, and some hung from polished steel hooks for Her Fury to wear.

There was a gallery of fountains, large vats of an unknown metal, housing water, blood, wines, and choice beverages from every nation of the continent, filtered through the petrified corpses or living bodies of men, for the queen and the Isscaran to drink from outstretched indera. The vats were hoisted high on support structures attached to wheels of a material I had never seen before, solid yet soft, limber as flesh, and leather to the touch. From the vats, the bodies of men lie at an angle with pipes planted inside their mouths, into their throats, so the fluids can pass through. Their interiors were emptied of all natural organs and replaced with configurations which allowed for fluid to fill the body and emerge from the indera when the scrotum was squeezed. Like others before them, legs were cut off at the hip, and a large suture seared shut from sternum to pelvis, made evident their inner-workings.

There was even a section devoted to collected indera alone, carefully laid out on tables of glass and resin. They were there for her to observe, admire, examine, and play with at any time. It was in one moment that she held one for me to see. She held it like the hilt of a sword, just beneath the scrotum with the length down so we could observe where the skin was cut from the body. With a proud gaze, she said in a whisper of arrogance, ;; *I did that. I'll always do that. It pleases me.* ;;

Elsewhere, there were ribcages torn open by her hands with faces and pieces of limbs stuffed inside. A great sculpture she crafted there, of flesh upon flesh, torso upon torso, heads and limbs squished together as though some cancerous growth, and adhered by mortar of her own make – a slimy, dripping sludge the color of sand. Rotting bones where everywhere, and bodies hung with the entrails above, disfigured, bleeding, dismembered, and pain-stricken faces staring at any who might see, whether the dead had eyes or not. Some of them lived, ever alive to fill the hall with whimpers of pain.

There are sculptures of living men, petrified in mangled pose, wet with blood that will not dry, having been sliced and carved by her nails. The art of it all, was found in the grooves and curves of the lines she scored into them, trenches of red meat, ground up, squeezed, and dug into by her vicious claw.

There is also a special sculpture, one that for reasons unique to her, she requested devoted women to volunteer as subjects – as clay. It is a sculpture made of many women, stripped of skin, or skin and flesh torn by teeth and nails, some missing limbs, and all with disfigured faces, to form a weeping woman on her knees with her head held in her hands. It stands at twelve lexims. Their hair was used to form her hair, still attached to their heads, and soaked in blood.

There is a pile of intestines and muscle, fifteen lexims high, formed into a large monstrosity of mass, as though a person excessively heavy. A kind of head is fixed upon it, with a wide, open mouth from which pour out more intestines mixed with blood and various organs. This outpouring reaches the floor.

Affixed center of the room, is the only sculpture made of clay from the earth and overlaid with gold. It is a reconstruction of her own oriva, thirteen lexims tall. The detail was precise. There, we stopped for a time, so she could admire its presumed beauty. Steps encircled its base so we could walk inside its depth. There was, unsurprisingly, a mound where she could lay me down, and of course, she did. She bace our flowings to fall where they might.

Anything the queen desired to see, is there – a house of horrors unto itself. It was another place of meditation for Her Fury. She walked this hall, amazed at all her handiwork, in love with her vision of death. She at once held my hand while we walked – a graceful tour of her craftsmanship, and she, my guide. She spoke softly. With awe and wonder she serenaded in pleasing tones, echoing an assumed majesty to her creations. She mentioned the works of her Isscaran, who proudly contributed living sculptures of men subdued by women. The women were stripped of skin and bathed in blood, having teeth filed with eyelids bleeding from punctured pupils.

At times, she stopped to hold me from behind, either a lover or a mother, swaying as if by music inspired. She would reach her hands through my garments, slipping into cloth as though merely a cloud, and stroke my front side from chest to waist. A massage of the loins came next. She would not allow me to withhold the release of fluids, and laughed when I resisted. It was mine to learn to separate mind from feeling, to understand that what I felt, was not what I intended, and then to understand that none of it mattered at all.

She used what was mine to anoint the floor as we walked. My blessing she desired, whether I did or not. Nevertheless, I wrote of her deeds as always, and before I rested for quiet, she took my blessing, whether I desired it or not. There never was desire, for none of it mattered at all. Though, that night, she turned me about on her bed before finishing me, to feel every part of my being with her hands, squeezing and kneading as the sculptor, closing her eyes and swaying with the flow of feeling.

I realized in all our time spent, there was one work of art, one trophy, which stayed with her at all times. Her foremost reason for showing me that hall, more than for me to remember it on her behalf.

At the end of the gallery, the part of the hall where light ceased and darkness seemed to go on forever, the queen had raised another vision of her oriva to dress the walls before the dark, itself an entrance to what lay beyond. The material of the make was like her own flesh, as her oriva magnified, expanded to fit the walls, and soiled with saturation. At its center was where the darkness dwelt. As she stared inside, she said to me in soft wandering tones, ;; *Where do you think it leads? Where by thought and thunder and perennial refuse, exists in there? Is it so mysterious, or as near and conspicuous as our eyes? Can you see the woman? beyond the woman? Is she so far…or near? Do you see her here – only here? ;;*

To this, I replied, "Only if I look in one direction, your fury."

To that, she smiled with wide eyes.

Care, I took in that hall, for there, more than anywhere else, my vision filled with horrors of the mind, growing louder, more impulsed, more violent the further we walked. The horrors were never my own. It seemed, memory had its own place amongst her trophies.

I speak present and past here, because this hall still exists in her new home, lovingly recreated to much wilder extremes. I am grateful, to be spared that sight. Though, if I desire it, I have but to open the doors.

I once asked her outright, why she did what she did, beyond what she put to the world as her vision. What was the core of her motivation? Her response to me was first a broad smile with wide, glowing eyes of orange. But as she thought, her smile slowly dimmed to a placid disassociation, then to say,

;; I don't know. All my boldest reasons bear a truth beyond knowing, or beyond longing, and beyond me. From their origin, I see no stars. All is absent the records of wild imaginings. All that I love, all that I believe, is woven together. Who will unravel the bond for me? If they unravel it, will they not die? Let them die. Then I will live. What truth is found in my answer, Hepatsu? Do you speak to me or another? No one can care, for to care, is to die. ;;

CHAPTER 10

RICHES OF RITUAL

If it is worship the Red Queen desires, then it is worship she shall have. I warn you, those who read, you know by now that Gishona was not beyond child cruelty, but the following portion may pierce the soul. I will spare much detail for the respect of innocence, though there be no innocence spared here.

For the Red Queen, many young boys you know were meat for meal in the time of sacrifice. But those not of Issacre, were not to be afforded the same courtesy. Hundreds were taken between the ages of five and nine, all to be, shall I say, mothered, by her. But not as a mother would.

A secret desire stirred in her, one which left her dripping with joy. In every land, on the same day, at the same hour, she gathered them together in a room not unlike her red hall, with a stepped pedestal in the center. Upon it, she stood with her junior multitudes surrounding her, holding the hands of some, a gleeful smile on her face, and taught them. She taught them to worship her. She taught them how to touch her, what to say and how, where to be and when, where and how to stand, to sit, to lay.

She made them her acolytes. They recited her words:

"In veneration, we lay our souls down before you. Our eyes are on you. They see you in your beauty. Our nostrils take in your life-giving breath and the scent of your silent song of love. Our lips receive you. They speak of the bounties of your radiance, your power, and of our desperation for

your blessings. Our tongues taste of your gifts from above, of your passions divine. Our hands feel what they cannot fathom. Our skin trembles with your fire. You are ever beyond us, yet you are with us. We can never attain your wisdom, your power, your greatness. We cannot imagine the fullness of your limitless wonder. Our thoughts cannot contain you. We are weak before you. Our bodies belong to you. Our minds are the fruits of your mouth. Our souls are yours to weave and wear. To love you is to be shattered by you, in the hope that we might one day be remade in your image, for we are broken before you and unworthy of your justice. You live forever, unfading, unyielding, supreme above all. All praise the Red Queen! All fear Her Fury! From the depths of your soul, long for her! All men bow! All the earth surrenders! Praise the Red Queen above all else! Praise the Red Queen above all!"

They recited this at the beginning and end of every meeting. The Bleeding Sacrima, she called it. They sang to her a song they scripted themselves, inspired by her influence.

Praise the Red Mother, lover of blood

Bask in her golden glow,

Take in her roses, scent of love

Be tamed and brought low.

Lay your tongue bare before her,

In her light, your frailty shows,

Surrender all,

Surrender all,

Surrender all,

Surrender.

Only in surrender may we rise,

Only to her ankles are we worthy,

Barely might we reach her knees,

Barely might our eyes perceive,

Pray she comes to meet you,

Pray she comes to see,

Pray she comes to make you,

All you're meant to be.

There were offerings, so many offerings. I must not say. For the next six years, she raised them to be her emissaries in the earth. Guided by an army of women trained in similar ways, a covenant of watchers, the children were dispersed overseas, to the unknown. Their mission: to prepare the way for the queen's hands to capture the rest of the earth. The queen's watchers had her power and pieces of her mind. A great reckoning was inbound, as far as she was concerned.

Forgive my brevity here in this part. It weighs heavy on me. A foul thing for me to suggest, but perhaps death would have been better for these so young, groomed for a lifetime of corruption.

I mentioned a covenant of watchers. There were many. Always nine to a fold. In ritual ceremony, they were endowed with their queen's life essence. The queen would hover above whilst they surrounded her in a nine angled formation, each the tip of nine sides, and she would release her energy like rivers flowing through the air into each of them. These were women who worshiped the Red Queen with a child's gleeful innocence and obsessive devotion, loving her body as though her personal slaves.

With the queen's power so radiant within them, she could see through their eyes and they could speak her mind. They smiled often, eyes blazing red, and spoke with a steady, smooth innocence, the voices of charm, honey to the ears, such that even a strong mind could be turned against itself in moments. Through them, Gishona's voice commanded obedience – total subjugation.

Their hands dripped with her power, always wet with blood, marking everything they touched. Blood oozed even from their eyes in the form of tears, and from their lips, coating them in crimson, and leaking a steady stream down the middle whenever they spoke, revealing a red-coated inner mouth. They could move the earth at will, whether land, sea, or otherwise, even the body, all by division and force, as were the queen's ways. They smelled of many roses, warm spices, and convolutions of pheromones designed to overtake, smother, and soothe the senses into agreement with the queen's will, or that of the women. The will of any member of the fold and of their queen was often indistinguishable. Upon the forehead of every woman was a mark exclusive to her, discolored and fused as by branding iron, and they wore robes which completely covered their bodies, save for their eyes, hands, and feet. I thought this an odd choice for a queen who prefers to proudly bear all before any who see her. These covenants were called, the Diamet.

CHAPTER 11

HER TONGUE

CX11

How do you interpret a mind unsafe for comprehension? You don't. You interpret the actions which follow such a mind. This will give you what you need to know, where interpretation is too volatile to take in. As with extreme conditions, it better serves us to take shelter from extreme forces of consciousness which thrive in chaotic tones. Yet, even in this wise, I am the stone which survives those extreme conditions, remaining still as storms pass over me and by me, inscribing weathered words upon my flesh, that I may provide a lasting means of comprehending the otherwise incomprehensible, long after the storms have gone. What knowledge would we have of the ancients, were it not for the stones they left behind to survive them?

So now to you, I divulge the tongue of the Red Queen, her words whose meaning might skewer any mind made to fully comprehend her multitudes of chaotic tones. These she proclaimed as they occurred to her, from her throne while the sun burned, and at times while the moon loomed in the lingering cold. Her voice, by her own will, echoed freely throughout the air, its resonance mighty as the gong so that all in Patashan could hear, as if she stood in front of every person.

The Words of Gishona, Red Queen of Patashan

For these first sayings, there is no specified audience, as it was expected that those who heard them understood by their contents, for whom they were intended.

;; I am the light which burns red a brazen sun to sear all beneath my radiance. Look on me and know my fury, for in me are the volumes by which you live and die. Bask in my light without shade, and know the strength I breathe into you. Hide from me and be consumed by it, my untamed appetite. ;;

;; To worship me is to know your place in this world. Be meat willingly, give yourself to my teeth, my tongue, my throat, my bowels, and I will restore you in my new world. ;;

;; You worship me in being, you who are strong by my fury. You bear in you my ways, my rage, my will, my mind, my longing, and my dominance over all other existing things. ;;

;; I eat the soul and the soul feeds me. Satisfy me, little soul. Let my teeth rend you sundered. Let my life-force capture and consume you, whereby you become me, and are made whole, new, complete in my image. ;;

;; I am the womb which births the world, a bloodline to bear all that is in me and become the indomitable aspect of change. ;;

;; The man is broken, frail in solitude, in his own company. For what is man without woman? Can he birth the world of his own effort? Has he the all to bear the living into the world? Has he value beyond the mineral deposit we, the woman, claim to ferry the fledgling ashore? ;;

;; Come all men to my breast. Let me teach you the value of pain. Let me show you your worth. Come to be bound. Come to be shattered. Come and let your filth be cleansed in brokenness. I will tear, claw, bite and bludgeon, your bones crushed and ground to make you clay for my hands. Rejoice! Your pain is my pride. In it, your truth is made vivid. ;;

;; Come all women and be free of the weights which hold you in contempt. Let go the man-molded shackles, lose all sense of pity, sacrifice all maternity, burn empathy for the lowly and useless until its ashes dissipate, and become strength in me. ;;

;; Let all bear witness to the might of the womb-bearing. ;;

;;Fear, oh man. Fear me. Fear my hands and the weight of my fingers as I crush your bones, make loose liquid the bulk of your form, my nails as I carve myself into you. The more of you I take, the more you become me. ;;

The Twelve Wisdoms:

;; Twelve wisdoms. Twelve wisdoms, I give to you, men of the waste, women of the great, and children of clay:

1. Walk to me in terror. Let me see your fear. If you do not, I will terrify you.

2. Bow before me and lie prostrate the ground. Turn on your back in submission to me and receive what I give you from above.

3. Drink from my streams and be anointed by my golden glow. By this, I will hear your voice.

4. If I select you for meat, render yourself silently to me. By this, I will devour you swift and you will suffer less. Debate, and you will suffer more by the hour for every utterance in defiance of me.

5. At all times, be ready to die. Death is your right, and long suffering is your passage into death. How long the suffering is mine to decide. Do what you can in obedience to lessen your pain, but know that nothing shall be withheld from me.

6. Worship me. Look upon my body and long for its blessings. Wish, want, and grow wild with passions. In your fear, let me see your desperation for me. If you are neither desperate nor wanting, I will draw them out of you.

7. Feed my fighting women willingly. Give them your souls in full surrender. Show them your vulnerability. By this, you may earn the chance to live and become strong like them. Yet, always remember your place beneath them, or your strength will crumble as dry leaves in their hands and they will be your long punishment.

8. Women of the world, surrender your souls to my cause. All your cares, your love, your trifles of charity, your desire to hold and be held, your maternity, all of it to me. These trivialities no longer serve you. My power will – my life-force.

9. Be strong in me, women of the great, and fear not death but give it, fear not pain but use it, fear not fear but let it feed you, and fear not the ill for you are stronger than it. Fulfill your rage in me. Bear it in your bosom. Let it be born again always in your womb.

10. Women of strength, let no one conquer you. If a challenge you find, find the path to victory, and let it forever be branded in your memory, a thread of blood flowing through you. Be the supreme lexicons of domination, until all others come to heel.

11. Intended matrons, selected for motherhood, bear me daughters for the great. Bear me sons for the waste. Rule your houses with pride. Prepare your daughters for suffering unto greatness. Intended fathers, submit to your wives and your daughters. Teach your sons the laws and love of the Red Queen. ;;

12. …..

The twelfth, I will not share, for what it demands of the child is everything. Its tones, for all the horrors made plain in this script, should neither be read on these pages, nor recited in the mind. Of all the wisdoms, it is most involved.

The Red Queen's private musings – that which only I heard.

;; Do you know my fury, Patashan? Do you know why I burn and boil – erupt? (Now in whispered tones) Do I know? What do I know? Where are you, malignant starlight which evades me? Where do you begin that my dreams are of distant suns beyond the scope of any lone body of dust? ;;

This one she speaks in weeping rage.

;; Come to me, great volumes of obscura, leaking pages of scrolled lexicons which true tell and lie deep. You tear and you train and you terrorize. You empty, fill, and empty and make full again. You crack me open, an egg shattered and light spilling into inordinance. Many voices make multitudes of maelstrom magics of unknowns. (Now in anguished screams) Why do you waste me? You love me! You have nothing for me! Where is my gift? Where are my loves? You! Why are my dead? Living ones dead! Where? ;;

;; Waste! Waste! Waste! Livings gone! Tear apart! Putrefy and eat! Pry open and plague! Bleeding! ;;

Bear your thoughts carefully here.

;; Betrothed. Dark, arid risen veil vast. Blind me and take my body bare. Forfeit me unaware – betrothed. Dark light in empty spaces, serene and soiled, broken and boiled, slain and slaying songs of lurid longings, visions unbound and unbearable, frayed and frail. Force in me melting and malcontent, slay me and force me to being. Be kind and brutal, bereave my soul, make me happily fool's blood for fragile minds distilled in distant tomes too vast and too many to make words measured whole.

Level your love, mountains low beneath themselves, invaded and disturbed, ovulating ova emasculating matured mired milk. Devastation devast, dirty and diving deep to lover's hold, old and new and never knowing why or who. Find me in ethers unfolding flight, fidgeting paler by heroes might, thrown beyond bright bloody moons to iron guards and untold soons. Failure frail and fraying out to horizons near, the best of what we all fear.

Are we fortified against water's loving light? Do we see with fledgling holes of absent sight? Cinders, cinders, hook and keys, kept from all this, lies to me. You found me not, you found me here, you found what love in charges spear.

Do you know the raging of my mouth? In great surges of sputum, red and writhing, leaking and leaping do I bellow and boil bruised and brazen speech. Pry and pierce with my aged teeth tarnished and gold, razors raised to raise all beneath their quaking crash, thunderous is their gnash, rip and tear, taunt, tatter, break and shatter. Show me light great crystals of night, long phalanxes of fiery fades and fallen shades. My tongue is the trap to draw all the dark inward dripping fools, dance with them in multitudes unmade. What did you to me? Tear my lover's gate gone, her fury mourns my lips dry, their towers crumble and deny. Have I fallen behind mangled eyes squeezing my body? Flesh pressed between orb and liquor, my inner undying dither, my rape of every part of me, therein for all her eyes to see, they fail never to look at me where I hide exposed to all yet never found.

Found? Found a golden light so piercing radiant battled bite. Blitz to me blazes of prying shards shaven and shaving wonders hard. Hard to scold, hard to have, hard to slow death and wailing slain alive. Bear down on me a golden key and set me free. Save me and call my name, by this I reach you rage and pain, to kill my soul unfilled and old to eat you whole swallowed and burned. I hate. I hate. I have no hate but never doings all encompassed, asking all for nothing and nothing for everyone. Wailing family wakes, waiting fire takes and tire, we three tire for all and take all things into ourselves. What sacrifice? Was there worth starry scores sour, sore and soaring wild with passions piled bled filled with endless nothings and stirred by outer nothings, outer knowings, reasons by rare diamond sparks, sprinks, spores, spiders and hoars.

Have me my gated flesh fly by blood waters pour! Rage and roar white, unintelligible elegance of weared whittled spires of soul sounds and volumes molded mightier than message! Take my fleshy feast! My skin to stretch, sew together and wretch, tare down and heave, have more and leave! Let the blood soak, boil and simmer, salivating sirens and songs of suns be gone. Fume up in puss, bile and bust, blessed slivers of slick slacking sludge, savory and sublime. I lick you up until you're mine.

What did you do to me, haphazard dark infused with measured molded arts unmeasurable, masterful, storms stink with smog and cinders? Tear into me with eyes, with pupils gut me grow back my millioned mind. So much milk drips through the cracks, an orbital appalachian affluence of barren mass cut by cruel crusts and crevasses. Spill out great milk and fall to ruin or righteous revolt against me.

Lights linger in song, burning my all and all I love but whence was mine for mine sake, service me and make me take the tired way home, bring about my servitude to self, loathed and alone. Broken I bind me free of death released and resealed, sold to the un-me, more me than I, more I than naught, there's nothing left but me and her.

Who is she? Who is her? Why does she laugh? This one laughs. This one loves. This one weeps for never enough. That one hates. Another hoards. Those few beat and break and board. They scour the stars for night to bring no light but things of stuporous haphazards loved and long gone. Lust me lately and seal my breasts for sundering, my knees for blundering your eye. I see all of you after the ire is out. Where is your dire flame now? When will you join me? When will you love? When will I be good enough? Enough for you? When you see me, what do I show you? What do we want from her? And where is he to satisfy the her beyond the him and the all?

I sucked you in, you two twain, swallowed and made you me. I squeezed you breathless in my bleeding fingers, punctured you with razors deep inside, made you as clay for simple minds and held you taught with chains to bind. I made you and made you unmade to serve the great maiden horde for hapless means of having all to me. You were mine. Where did you? Where to be? My eyes. My bosom. My knees. My stones for seeing silver slight. I'll find you again.

Where time deceives all by make true, I make my simple slaves of you, great purges practical in undenied tenders of tapestry, recorded for all to see yet hidden from divine deceivers who love to play the palpable, binding all to bitter sweets and barren beats, bold flow fools false and falsely flattered flagrant flits. Fire away from me and yourselves twain and twitted. The wires of where and how and who, coil all of you for meat and hook. Now you cook for fires grace to make more space to fill you with forms you do not know. Fashion with syllables ever by the sybils of sublime missives to appease and peel away the perverse for more perverse parody of ovum's paradigm.

One light. One more languished light. I see you. Your eyes always on me. I don't fear you. You never owned me, never knew me, you... remind me of...you know something...where is that something here? Why don't you come near? Why don't you fold me in? burrow deep beneath my skin? My skin. My skin. My skin. ;;

This is a collection of conversation which goes on and on for many nights at a time, like seasons of storm upon the sea, a phenomenon I had never seen in person then. I know it now. To feel the earth change in volumes of water is an experience I most cherish. But in the Red

Queen, such stirrings should never be fathomed. Nevertheless, there's something in her mangled speech. Something.

These next words to my ears spoken, as she imitated love to me. She drew in close, her voice tender, soft, and dominant, her lips near my skin or touching, so I could feel her words inside me.

;; I know you, Hepatsu, and you are mine. By this voice you were made, the same voice which commands your body to cry out to me. Here within my walls, you lay, always my silent, unquenched flame, undying, unspoiled by all that spoils, incorruptible…and truly mine. I formed you. I made you from sad king to finest of men. Your eyes are mine. Your lips are mine. Your ears are mine. Your nostrils are mine. Your throat is mine. Your chest is mine. Your belly is mine. Your hands, your arms, your knees, your legs, your feet, are mine. Your hips and your untrained scales are mine. Your back and your entrails are mine. Your soul is mine. All of you belongs to me. Now and always. ;;

;; Let your body shout my name. Feel me swallowing you whole when I am not near you. Let your thoughts bear the weight of my flesh. My words, my image, your dreams. Let your flesh breathe my air. Feel me creeping, grasping every part of you until only I exist. Let no other claim what I have subjugated. I deserve all your being. You rise and fall to me. ;;

Here, she was soft and impassioned, though relaxed – rested.

;;How was it your perfection evaded me? Your little flame? You were lonely and unloved. Only your unpruned memory accompanied you. How did you gain such a long, flowing mind that I did not see? I knew you before you were born. I was your shadow. I made sure that none could claim you, save me. Yet, I did not see your mind. Did you not see me spying you? You sent me a sign from far away, and from a great distance, I saw you, your souls calling out to me. So I came in a hurry to nurture you to my own soul. ;;

I received mixed signals from her account of spying and knowing me before I was born. And...what sign? In all my memory, I do not recall sending her a sign, especially one whereby I beckoned her to me. She spoke of souls, not of one, but more than one. It seemed, her own memories were entangled, as much a thicket as her soul. Who is she? I wondered then.

This next moment was a change for her. She was at once unsure of who I was to her, with a hope that seemed out of place. She is one who eroded all such subtleties in flames of fury. Nevertheless, this she said:

;; You are my Hepatsu. Always laced around my neck – the jewel that rests where all can see. But only you touch me. Hepatsu. My dearest Hepatsu. Could you love me? Do you, love me? ;;

To this, I answered, no. I could not lie to her.

She, with the tenderness of a child, asked why.

I said, "You did not select me for love, but for memory, proud of your deeds, believing that the world should know. You have seen to the pleasures you believe should be acceptable to me. But you do not know me. You therefore cannot treasure who I am. I am to you as you have said – a jewel, laced around your neck. A jewel, cannot love its bearer, and so, neither can I."

In the same softness, eerily innocent, this, was her reply.

;; Oh. I, I thought maybe...It is naught. I will be alone for a while. ;;

I thought perhaps she would react with untamed anger, even towards me, but she instead fell to melancholy, as one humbly beset by some missed opportunity. That there was any such humility at all, gave way to the appearance of an other Gishona, instead of the conniving, raging Red Queen. Who was this now?

I called out to her, saying, "My queen?" I walked over to her and held her hand. I said, "My dearest Red Queen, for all your wrath and ruin, is this truly what plagues you?"

I led her back to the bed. We sat and I held her for a time. What was the meaning of this, that I should hold in tenderness, a monster? Had I endured all her masterful torment of an entire continent so I might discover this? as though having excavated the depths of the earth to find a single uncut crystal? And could any other man in Patashan reach this moment, even in the whole of the world? Perhaps. But, for now, it had to be me. Whether this turned her toward a path of healing, or she continued in her monstrosity, this moment happened. This potential exists. She could not undo it.

Whether or not she is in any way redeemable, relies entirely on fully understanding who she is and how. Yet, what sort of mind can reach her that way? What sort of mind can see? Somehow, we must learn to understand her being, or else the danger to our world will far exceed the possibility of redemption.

Many more passions did she preach in her self-gratification. As I recall them, I will list them here in the text.

CHAPTER 12

THE GREAT REMINDERS

CX12

These meanings will be understood by those who read, according to how ready they are to receive. Some are good for comprehension in the moment. Others, are good for comprehension after much meditation and experience. Even if a concept is universal, its truth might only be unveiled by the variance of individual context.

Do not feel compelled to agree; agreement is not understanding. Challenge them if you must. It is better for some to disassemble within the safety of their own thoughts, before they arrive at the lesson within. By this, they may extract a finer bounty. If to you these meanings are mirrors, then know yourself that much more.

All is well with you, always.

Love is all around you. Love is in you. Love is you.

You are, in all things, the finest incarnation of yourself. Any opposing message is not found in love. What confounds us are the identities to which we bind ourselves, which convince us otherwise.

Though many things challenge our resolve, oft to divide us from ourselves and turn us to want and wickedness, we can remember that we were and always are whole beings, only as divided as we choose to be.

We have help always, ever connected to minds more expansive than our own, while we remain limited in this hollowed partition. Understand, it is not our connection that is limited. We, therefore, need not be limited either.

Do not be slowed by the siphoning of time. Remember that we are ever present, and the gates of past and future will dissipate into the ever-flowing continuum of our present moment.

Remember how good you are. Even in our presumed darkness, the truth of our goodness can make pure and invite unyielding clarity, should we choose it.

A world which curses you for perceived faults, rather than to aid you in remembering your goodness, does not desire that goodness. Tune your thoughts to the songs of unyielding love.

If goodness is desired, then there is no such thing as fault or failure. The problem and the solution cannot coexist. Either we choose the problem, the fault, the failure, or we choose the solution. Solutions are always available to you.

What you agree with, you empower, even when you appear to be oppressed. Choose your agreement. You can always choose.

It may seem just to condemn and malign those we consider wrong. Yet, what solution do we offer in our condemnation? Is it not a finer thing to remind them of their goodness always, and provide a continuum of solutions? By this, we do not feed want and wickedness, instead giving love a habitat in which to thrive.

We experience love in its purest form, but fear of its loss poisons that purity.

Fear, if allowed, divides us from clarity, from our connection to the continuum, convincing us that the solutions we always have, never were. It is after the storm of fear passes that we realize its deception.

By submitting to fear, we empower it. By fighting fear, we feed it, focus on it. Do not fear this cycle. Simply choose your agreement and remain attuned by that choice.

If aggressors cause you to feel powerless, rejoice. For your inner being knows that this powerless feeling is appropriate. How? It tells you everything you need to know about your aggressors. The feeling of powerlessness is never your weakness, except you receive it. It is an indication of their want for power. Those who want it, have fully agreed that they do not have it already. By targeting you, they admit that you have it.

If a thing is true, none need coerce you to believe it, whether you believe it or not. If any attempt to force you, they do not believe it themselves.

Force nothing. Plant your crop in the finest conditions, and leave it to sprout its own shrub.

As dams to rivers of water, too much control, and its want, hinder the natural flow of the continuum. Do not fear to let go.

If all energies in the collective cosmos cannot die, only change, then we are, of course, endless, reincarnating in other forms, as water becomes vapor, and vapor, clouds, and clouds, rain, and fire, fumes, and earthly bodies, soil, and all things, the cosmos.

For all energies to be endless, also means that we happen again, that we have happened before, that all things come round in the continuum. How then might we believe death to be the end?

Yes, you can love everyone, if you remove from love the shackles of sacrifice. By sacrifice, I mean to expend one's life in service to others, beyond what is necessary and beyond personal well-being. There must be balance between your needs and that of another, so that love remains a flowing river, rather than a dry lakebed. Then you can disseminate love according to how much of it is ready to be received. If it is not ready to be received, then by this, you relinquish nothing. Let it be.

Love cannot be earned. That which must be earned is not intended for you to have, from the inception of cost. But if love is the language of the cosmos, then it is at all times without a price, and none can be placed on it, save what we convince ourselves there must be.

CHAPTER 13

HER TONGUE: PASSION'S PRIDE

CX13

;; Our love was passionate and proud, we triministrata, loud and looming.

By languished longings of my teeth, I sundered strange and strangled cords, opulent fruits brimming with delightful solutions, red and juice-filled flowing and spurting, gushing liquor from testines inside swollen bellies bare. That sinew should taste so rare, so delicate, delicious as countless tones of whipping strands meet baubles of sense and savor, teaching them to love overwhelmed by smothering wash.

I slipped and slurped their loving juices, slid across bone and tendons tight – my tongue's delight. My lips love the long sinking ships of skin on rising bloody tides within, my banquet great and engorging. To tear and trouble by gripping razors bid my nostrils perfumes of wretched scent by thousands spent, spittle spattering all about my body bare, roaring demons dark they dare. In waves of wonder I saw them in the tear so black.

I eyed endless hollow wall, a world of doomed recall and all dead, and all dying, and all raging and writhing and crying and killing, scoring and scorching by wet loving oils, sewage entwined, tired and shrilling, tasting of tales made millioned and horrid beauty.

I beheld them in love and loved them with wet drippings, taking all for shame and sorrow to be as they were and are and never. Night incarnate where light squanders, stilled by violent endlessness ever released upon withered welfare and wild whims. Joy and fury fastened by smite, might of old angels of living bodies make, mild men and mo (other beings) peoples from paler and brighter worlds. Behold the humata (humankind) is small and smells of weak wilterings putrid and petrified by holes in every seam. Same ones for same syllables ever by the sybils of sublime missives to appease the masses mired in childish chimmers chafed, wanting of waste to devour. My delight and mighty hour.

I bathed with them, I bled with them, these dim beasts the wall of hollows and endless. I gave them offerings of pain and pleased their ire to love what they lose and love losses all. Lost in them, I gave dreams their minds to speak of sliced silver, for they would cherish all benigns to spread the warmth of their dire substance until all mirrored them, refracting frailty and mighty dark loomings, holes and hollows, draining waters drooling into my mouth.

The lips of mine which speak beneath my horizons spit and spatter living thought and children hated high, life of the dead defying all I am and was and all. They love me yet they fall…And so do I.

My two, my lovely two. My twain. I have failed fruitless in you. You in me. I twisted you too deep. I made you there to sleep your minds to slave for my indecency divine. I ravaged you rolled and ruled you whole and burnished you brides of my many folds. I held you denied of breath and blood-filled bliss. I made you…into this. Where are you now to Void Mother's moanings? Can you not see me stoned? Sitting for you is lesser for me to wait for your lost charity. I miss the triministrata, we three. I miss us all for what we need. I knew something there beyond our walls. I knew what fillings failed recall. Where are you now? I doomed us all. ;;

CHAPTER 14

THE HOT SEASON

"For mercy binds us to bitter finds, where righteousness searches for meager signs, all to reach a single solid mount, on which to cast away all doubt, and let roll into the steep below, the pains of life which burden us so."

I speak these words in volumes never ceasing, ageless, full and unbound in context and ransomed rights. What came to us, a new year's gift hailed from her high fury, was a wave of devastation deeply disemboweling. The hot season. Eraquine (Erak-queen-ay) Herrosis, she called it. The deed which undid us all.

This language was of her own make. A basis we did not understand. Yet it was spoken aloud by her Diamet, four factions of nine, gathered in a deep temple, where they worshiped their queen, and with her, spoke these foul tomes:

Aquinat, diamot, drekasis. Nemsos nil arrad. De-hiacos num, de Eraquine Herrosis coma dan. Tempte nansonil, Gishon katwik queneda mol, foretu, faralas, aquinat diamot.

Direct translation of their utterances is a lesser feat than what they produced. From nostrils, breath, eyes, and fingers, rose red smoke as birthed by funeral pyres, dispatched from the temple depths to the surface. From there, the soil cracked and crevassed to release fumes into the sky where great was their gathering. A cloud to cover all Patashan.

Great red fumes clustered like the plumes of Mt. Haladine to the north, so thick they appeared solid and alive, shifting and rolling as waves of the sea. Lightning coursed through them like veins, illuminating what otherwise seemed a hardened hide. The volume of the clouds made stiff the air, trapping heat and moisture between sky and land.

A storm blew through, like the desert sands, dry and tumultuous with cutting speed. It came from the Northeast and spiraled around the continent along its outer regions, making way to its center. It brought the fullness of hot air to reign in the new season.

There was a clearing, near the crater of Balashah – the Valad Hiyel (High-yell) valley – her favorite spot. A desert region of many miles all around, once an oasis in its entirety. There, was the crown of the hot season. In this place, great rains of molten fire scorched the earth, forming lakes of lava flows and long patches of burning ground unsafe for travel. All other ground, though not hot enough to burn flesh, was nevertheless uncomfortable to walk upon whether by shoe or sandal. The cities were simply unbearable for all, save the queen and the Isscaran. Breathing offered no respite, as the air in was as thick and hot as air out.

None were allowed to die from asphyxiation and exhaustion. But all were allowed to incapacitate and enter a state of low breathing, continually tortured by their condition, and always near death but never there.

Help, I have with this one – this memory. It is one that pierced my soul and gripped an arter (artery). My speech here edits for brevity of thought. Some of what I describe, you may have seen before.

I witnessed the queen gallop with joy on the hot ground, as if celebrating fresh rain following a drought.

Hundreds of thousands of men were taken from their homes, or dragged from prisons, stripped of their clothing and carried out to the waste.

She took one at a time. She dragged them on their backs against the hot ground, by a chain bound to their wrists. Her eyes blazed wild with joy as they screamed.

She forced them to walk upon lava beds. Their necks were chained. Their hands were chained. Their chests and waists were chained, all tied together and wrapped around with long extensions behind them and before them, so the queen and her women could pull them backward or forward from either end. They laughed as they pulled, gleeful as children.

Whilst windstorms roared and pierced flesh, the queen used her fingernails to rip men apart with wild strokes, one slash at a time. She stabbed them, crushed their bones with her hands until they became as paste that she could push about with her fingers, enjoying the nuances of tones in their moans as though tuning an instrument.

She went savage with her nails, clawing and mangling and digging into the skin, ripping slabs of flesh from bones, peeling it off muscle to either expose flesh to the open heat, or liquify the fresh meat between her fingers.

She tossed them into the air to her Isscaran. They caught them and threw them back, at times taking bites for every catch.

The Isscaran played with male subjects, pulling them apart, limbs from sockets, twisting and bending, stretching bodies through acrobatic collaborations, crushing heads between their knees.

They built large pulleys of metal for lowering men into lava lakes, and made them endure barbarity, sending them down with a gallery of open wounds, or completely skinned to red, bleeding flesh. They were not permitted to die, or even to burn severely, but only on the surface of their flesh, whilst they felt all the pains of molten consumption.

She beat them, the queen. They all did, the Isscaran. She took time to beat them with her bare fists until muscles were too weak to remain intact. She threw them about, slamming them against the ground, pinning their faces to searing sand until their skin burned sufficiently and smashed their faces against it with the utmost rage. What monstrosity, even for all that she has done.

She had iron hooks standing up from the ground, curving outward and folding over itself, into the horizon, as the head of a crested serpent (cobra), and tapered at the tip. The queen lifted a man by his waist and hoisted him into the hook, pinning him to its sharp end through his indera. An Isscaran assisted to ensure precise insertion, as though threading a needle.

A horrible joke on the queen's part, but that was not all. Once hooked, she pulled him back by his ankles while the Isscaran guided the tip of the hook through the indera until it breached the pelvis. Once there, the queen continued to pull until the tip split him down the middle, relieving his head of its divided lower portions. Two of the Isscaran used the split parts to beat other men, flailing the husks about by the ankles.

The queen's first exhibit of this act was an example she expected her fighting women to follow, and follow they did. They had their fun, twisting and mangling them to explore how creative they could be in its practice.

Lamentations of the Hunt

Isscaran recruits were brought out of the cities to walk the shallow spreads of fiery ground to further ingratiate themselves in the Isscaran way. Some did so willingly, and some willed not. There were hunting games in which recruits were charged to find certain men targeted for slaughter. The men were given the freedom to run for their lives. It was all fear and primal incentive to survive which willed men to run. Otherwise, they had not the energy as the heat drained it from them, making for laughable, easy prey.

Ah but there was more to it. As prey was tackled or dragged from behind by nails and teeth, a man looked upon the face of his attacker and saw his child, and she, her father. Stricken, her eyes blossomed a sudden wide blaze. She released him, anxiously removing the meat and blood from her teeth. She covered her mouth, her face breaking, squeezing streams from her eyes, shivering, as for a moment, her body knew not what to do. Then, a subtle calm. She was a daughter again. Father called out to daughter and daughter to father, both weeping and holding one another. This young woman, despite all things, treasured being held once more in love.

This was an offense. An offense for which they were both found and forced to watch each other torn apart by hungry mouths and devoured, though the woman only in part. After she watched her father's torment, she was forced to eat pieces of him before he died. She fought, as hard as she could. But she was absent a third of her flesh and quite weak, for all the strength she had gained by then.

The Isscaran reveled in forcing her father down her throat, laughing themselves silly at her struggle. Anyone else, she would have eaten immediately. But after their fun, they did something to her. They had developed a way to manipulate certain muscles in the body to inspire a state of starvation by which she would become too hungry to resist any meat they gave her. They pressed her forehead with the long finger, held her belly, squeezed her neck beneath the jaw, and placed two fingers inside her nostrils, holding her for several seconds. When that was done, they loosed her upon what was left of a man she once knew, and she finished what the Isscaran started.

Again, a man was caught in the hunt and after eating part of him, his pursuer beheld the face of her husband. She paused, eyes alarmed and searching, remembering a time when she was his wife. She held his face with a timid tenderness – a face which looked upon her in disorientation. His eyes squinted, then shared in alarm as he looked upon the hand that held him. He did not recognize her. She saw this, and all that was left was to let go – a final act of sorrow. Then she strangled and ate him.

Once more, a young man was pounced to the ground, a young woman on his back. When she turned him about to see his face, he called out, "Sister!" and she stopped. She trembled with a coldness about her face, lips tight and eyes sharply upon him, though avoidant. Her thoughts raced through many nights in which he went to her room while she slept, to take advantage of the only woman he felt he could. Her face darkened, lips remaining sealed, until she grimaced and said, "Brother."

He attempted to usher the faintest joy in relief, but his muscles failed as he felt himself turning over, and was stricken with horror the moment he felt his thighs bent upward and snapped at the hips. Amidst his screams, his sister rolled him onto his back to face her and broke his shoulders next. Finally, she sat upon him, eyes void of all affection, and said, "You will not struggle."

She delivered upon him what was forced upon her years before, but went further, slitting his flesh with her nails and causing him extensive pain every time she pressed her weight. She went on for hours in the hot land, forcing him beyond his limits, and the Isscaran gloried in it. They later joined her when she was ready, so they could feast together, beginning with a long kiss, whereby she reached in and chewed his tongue, eating it along with his lips. They gave her the honor of dining on his most vulnerable parts and his inner thighs.

Before he could die, the new recruit requested the queen imbue her once brother with her essence, so he could live. As soon as she uttered the words, the queen stood behind her, and gladly rendered her request approved. He was to be his sister's personal subject for as long as she desired. This pleased the queen to the point that she felt to stand over his face, moaning with delight, and released all fluids into the crater of his mouth. Those gathered with her, joined in. The young man's sister unleashed all excrement upon him, escalating the affair into a ceremony of devastating humiliation. The young man's wounds burned. His eyes burned. Just from ill-placed liquids irritating. But then was felt the heat of the air, and moisture boiling on his body, boiling his blood, and the added sounds of laughter from his captors standing over him.

You might believe that he deserved what was delivered upon him. But I have no such fathoms of judgment. In this climate, all men are made equal to one another. All peoples are made equal. Male, female, or otherwise, all are made monstrosities in the ire of queen Gishona, whether monsters enslaved, or monsters made mighty. Here and now, no punishment, even for horrid wrongs committed, is separate from another. No justice. True of all persons ruled by the Red Queen, if ever that young man could have had opportunities to mend his ways in years to come, those opportunities were now devoured along with the flesh he would never regain. That is, provided conditions remained this way.

So many men and women suffered similar encounters – a final test for Isscaran recruits to prove their devotion by deteriorating the last of familial ties. There could be afforded no setbacks. All love must perish in all its forms for the soldiers of the Red Queen to come alive.

End of Lamentations

The Isscaran, unfazed by the heat, laid men face-down or face-up on lava beds, and laid on top of them as though to rest, or please themselves upon them. They played with them, made love to them in imitation, and even piled on top of them. At times, they slept on them. As men were forced to stillness, their bodies boiling, so too did my soul boil and sear.

The queen was wild with gleeful monstrosity, a demon of chaos, contorting her face with a dazzling wide smile of bleeding razors, enlarged amber eyes aglow, and stressed skin. She crept and pounced about the Valad, hunting and ravaging her male subjects while they suffocated and suffered from the smothering swelter. She had moments of scattered passion, muttering and groaning to herself, letting excrement fall freely when and where she felt the need.

She drank lava from a pool, digging her face in it. With this bounty of fire, she held a man's mouth open and vomited down his throat through muffled screams and painful shivers, until vocal chords could no longer sound. The whole of the air screamed.

She also did something more sinister than all that came before, by my reckoning. As usual, she keeps those prisoners she intends to make suffer from dying. In this instance, she had a man inside a bowl-shaped brazier of iron, large enough to fit his entire body inside, save his head. Holding his head from behind, she released a dark red smoke from her hands that descended his body, filling up the brazier. To his horror, and mine, his body liquidated into a molten ooze, leaving his head and the remainder of his neck in the queen's hands. Because the ooze never cured, his body never stopped burning, and though it appeared he should not have been able to scream, scream he could, and scream he did, in new horrifying volumes which, by their very tones, urged me to vomit and scream at once. Yet I did not.

The queen then carried him to the other side where there was a spout attached to the brazier. She placed the man's head atop the edge above the spout and sealed him to it so he could watch as she laid upon the ground and drank from it, consuming his liquid form. She then kissed his lips and began to chew each time she extended her jaw after the first kiss. As she began to eat him, she stuffed her right hand into his head, through the neck as though a glove, and when she was done, sucked her fingers and licked what remained from her hands. Such foul tricks she was afforded by this strange power within her. Such foul, diabolical tricks, ensuring that there was no length she wouldn't go, unless by her whim, she refused to.

I walked the waste a disturbed man, ever sound in knowing that all was well with me, yet aching for having endured so long in the heart of madness whilst unable to relieve all those who suffered. After so many seasons later, I felt a desolation within me. Not merely a desire, but a need to let go, to no longer trouble the earth with my presence. As I stood in swirling, dusty winds, I closed my eyes, ready to leave.

It was then I felt something familiar, yet new, and I looked ahead to see a strange womanly figure clothed in a glow as that of heated metal, but brighter. Her form was as voluptuous as the queen's. At once she was afar off, and in an instant, face to face with me. Her face, though not much to it, was clean and slender towards the chin, lips full and healthy upon a wide smile, and eyes larger than most any human entity I had seen, with a bold forehead mantled by long, wonderous hair. She touched my face with her hands, and rested her head against mine.

From whence she came, I know not with precision, for it was never a concern, and so the answer never came. But she messaged me by lightning from her mind to mine, drawing my attention to the clouds above. To my eyes, they cleared the sky in respect of the universe dazzling with lights. So many houses. So many souls. So many friends.

I wondered why she could not help us, but then, as always, I understood. If we do not resolve this now, on this plane, then all will happen again in exponential splendor. She, Her Fury, will happen again. We have all we need here, though it seems not, but only because the aggressors do all to force us to see things their way, to convince us that what we have available to us, is not available at all. And if we do not use what we have here, we risk spreading that waste elsewhere in exponential splendor. It must be here. It must be now. And we can.

Moreover, I understood that for aggressors to claim power by force, is their admittance that they do not have it at all. An admittance that they do not even *believe* they have it at all. They must therefore convince all else of the same notion, so they appear to themselves to have what they willingly forfeit. They desire that all existence become a gallery of mirrors reflecting the image of power whilst they act the part, attempting to convince themselves that it is anything more real than an imitation of a reality they desire.

The queen saw me from afar, witnessed my head tilt toward the sky, and fell shattered by jealousy. To me she ran and pinned me to the hot ground, but not for the punishment of heat. With hands clenching my shoulders, she looked with rage into my eyes, still glowing with peace, searching them for answers. It was here with vengeance she inquired,

;; What do you see? What do you see that I do not? What there is hidden from me that would share with you so closely? ;;

Though it seemed she would do me harm at last, I understood much better. Yet, no sum of harm would change my answer to her.

"With the utmost respect, my queen, neither my eyes nor my thoughts can speak the lightning to thunder in your mind as it does in mine and incite waters to saturate dry ground. If I told you what I saw you would not know what it means, and nothing could make it so. You have chosen dry waste and clouds which produce fire and trap water, hindering its ability to replenish as it was made to do. You look upon enlightenment and say to it, no, eclipsing it with your need to control what it tells you. From it, your eyes hide, and so from you, it is withheld. But never because it is hidden from you…For nearly seven years, you've troubled me for answers I could not give. You knew I could not give. But you cannot stop yourself from demanding control of the answers. Truth cannot be controlled, but revealed. And only revealed, to those who are willing to receive it. We must receive truth to have truth, because, we too, are truth incarnate. To realize this, is to begin to understand our existence. But you want to control it, and so you grasp at air when all air can do is slip through your grasp, or around it. It is never stopped by you."

Her anger towards me was most furious. As much a storm as the raging of the hot season. Nevertheless, there was a discipline in her, for though all ceaseless wrath drove her, seething to erupt upon me, there was no such exhaustion.

She instead rose and walked away. Anything, she could have done to me that eve. But for the first time, I was to walk in on her, her back turned to me, motionless as a mountain. This time, however, it was that womanly being who bathed me lovingly, clothed me, and laid me gracefully in bed. And indeed, I felt love, both strange and familiar, yet healing to my soul. Queen Gishona never once turned her head. Such a strong presence. It was curious that she had no reaction to it. How could she not know? or at least feel? But then, as she learned prior, she hid herself from it. And perhaps now, hiding was more important.

Often in life, it is more important to us that we mind what we are running from, than whatever safety we intend to run to. This I knew well. I had born this mind many times. But no longer. Though I wondered…what is she running from? Does she know what she's running from? Does she know that she's running?

Some key observations: the queen is a scattered mind, oft echoing the remains of something left behind. She seems otherworldly, entirely unacquainted with human or humane custom. Separated; so very dis-integrated, as though a composite of disparate and fragmented individuals forced together in one soul, and that soul forced into human limitations, all fighting for control. Some react at different times in response to decisions made by one or another. Rarely do they agree, and rarely are they fully aware of themselves. Though, on this persona of horror, they seem very much unanimous.

In all of this, there is also a remembering of something, perhaps that world left behind. I didn't say so before, but I feel that's what it is. Some world…somewhere. Perhaps a here we do not know. Perhaps her disorientation is a symptom of displacement from this other world. Each disparate part of the soul remembers, however fragmented, however scattered. Something happened. I am not equipped to see that far, that deeply into her. Not in the limited instance of this identity. I would needs go beyond this to know, or some greater power meet me here to connect me to there, wherever there is.

Though, the more I think on this, the more my mind opens to a bright horizon, a promise of a great breadth released in forever tones of unceasing light. The answers which I am not equipped to process, may yet become clear to me, after all.

CHAPTER 15

THE AUTHOR

CX15

While I, her scribe, recorded her doings near and far, the Red Queen fashioned a red writ of her own. Its form, of many pages, long as an elder's forearm, two-thirds of that length wide, enclosed by a golden cover, saturated with blood that it might bleed red. It was made purely of her thoughts, forced into existence by her fury. By the same power, the gold bent where necessary for the cover to open and close as with any book. Its pages were refined leather to the touch, as though made of skin.

Contained therein, constricting cords forced into scripture, scratches and screeches entwined and bound to an unwilling landscape, desperate to erupt from its binding. Characters of language are so convulsed in their arrangement that no unaltered mortal mind known to me can withdraw meaning by sight. Yet, each strand translates to the mind according to what language best suits the reader within an instant of opening the book.

The queen, so proud of her craft, summoned a man of exceptional intellect to her chambers so he could read it. She would not risk blemishing her precious, prized Hepatsu. If only she knew, I did not need to. But this man, Iyad Rendi (Eye-yād, Rend-ee), she prepared for this. She kept him well away from her new and bloody civilization, in a mansion forged in an oasis, free from harm and horrors. She stayed with him there, treated him as a lover, with the utmost support of his studies in the sciences, causing him to feel much a king of a man. He thought her a goddess of all things good and came to know a version of her other-worldly power, having seen and received many gifts from her.

Now was a new gift – a next step in innovation – an opportunity to learn secrets of the universe…so he was meant to believe. She made love to him first, occasionally looking back at me with flaunting stares. It seemed I was something of a disappointment, as she clearly gained from him the enjoyment I failed to render. How silly for one to expect authenticity from imitation. Nevertheless, there was someone, loving authentically at the behest of her imitation. And then, with newfound excitement, his confidence amplified, he boldly opened the book with glistening eyes.

In a moment, his glister dimmed to darkened pearls behind strained lids. His forehead stained red beneath his skin with fractured veins. The whole of his face stressed frozen in anxiety. Sudden convulsions forced the book free of his hands. It levitated, keeping eye-level with him. He struggled to form words. His mind was overrun with thoughts as rapid rivers to a great fall. The book's pages seemed entangled with him by bleeding strands the width of pen marks, at first, barely visible, and increasingly visible with the advancement of his struggle.

Words of blood wrote themselves upon his flesh. His agony amplified, as did the queen's pleasure. His bones twisted and cracked. His muscles bulged and punctured, popping open slits of flesh flying across the room. In the end, Iyad burst into a holler. His flesh frayed, twisted and squeezed into figures akin to that of weathered rocks. And finally, he exploded.

The queen shrieked with a wide grin, flexing her fingers in the air and drawing all his scattered remains back into a human form on the floor. As he congealed, the man Iyad was gone, replaced by a sad, wailing, convulsing, corrupted mind, eyes white without pupils, each smothered by a thicket of red veins. His mouth was a cavity, cutting through the front of his throat where all housed within was now visible. The man was smothered in blood – opaque with it. There was no part of him distinguishable from another, neither in pigment nor configuration.

The queen moved her fingers again, reshaping his left arm into the tail of a crocodile, his whole body into a lump of intestines with a head, or a web akin to spider's silk. She turned him into a beast of many forms in one, all by causing him pain. At times, blood splattered and landed on her face, much to her pleasant surprise. She gladly extended her tongue and licked herself clean, savoring the taste. She then turned to me, grabbed my face, kissed me, and said,

;; I now have clay to mold and make new. ;;

Then said I, "As if you needed a book to rewrite what was already written."

She stared at me with a playful scrutiny, brows raised and a smirk. By her power over the elements, she thrust me free of my garments and onto the bed. The monster dormant, she leapt upon me and sat. As a time before, her hands were on my shoulders, though gentler. While she forced me inside her, she kissed me, breathing on my skin so I could feel her air. Her exhale was as the breeze before a storm. And then came the storm.

;; Are you disappointed in your work, Hepatsu? Is there something I can do to enlighten you? remind you of why you live? ;;

"No, my queen," I said, "My work is your will to remember, and you remind me of it every day."

;; Then what is it that disappoints you so deeply? ;;

Nothing could hide her threatening tones, but threat was no use here. To that, I said, "Is that a question to which you earnestly desire an answer?"

Upon my questioning, she stopped and said, *;; No. ;;*

She sat up beside my knees, cross legged and looking to the sun's light in her window before returning her gaze to me. Her words now were gentle, distant, even forlorn. And as she spoke, her gaze drifted from me to the sun's light and back to me, time and again.

;; I ask in rhetoris (rhetorically). I know how you feel about what I do, and what you think of me... I love the contrast. ;;

She stared for a long time at the light, silent. At last, she called my name, *;; Achmed ;;* a name she had not spoken in all of six years. What a strange turning.

;; You are here, and still so far off. she said, *I have captured all of Patashan, a cluster of worms full in my hands. I can reach in with my tongue and draw them to the devouring void at will... But you. I chose you. I made you. I prolonged your life, relieved you of need. And still, if I released you, you wouldn't... ;;*

Hmm, devouring void? I thought.

"No, my queen. I gather I would be further from you still."

;; Then why do you stay here? ;;

"Because it is not me who needs, my queen."

Her eyes locked on to me for a length of time. The wonder in those eyes. An intensity I could not describe. But dissect? Hmm. It was awe, but not. It wasn't anger or punitive intent. A tinge of longing. The mind sorting through a gallery of thought, or a thicket, for her part. Whatever its purpose, I could not know then, and I care less to know now, though I could if I but opened the door. Nevertheless, after her contemplation, she eased herself over me again and wrapped her body around mine, her head at my neck, her arms cradling my head.

I was paralyzed. I knew not what was the make of this mayhem. But fear offers only more of itself to those who entertain it. So it was useless here. I instead, exhaled and allowed the light of my being to soothe me inside. I hadn't consciously realized that light was now so palpable, but then, there was no need for conscious realization prior to that moment. It was important because I was now a danger to her. I felt that if I allowed that light to spread, she would be burned by it and have reason to overtake me in all the ways she has avoided thus far. And though I could escape with my life, she would do even worse to all the world for my offense. Escape was all there would be for me at the time. There was not yet enough energy like this in Patashan to stay her outrage.

The book. The book. The book…She, rewrote all manner of men and boys with it, making murals of fine art with flayed flesh on walls that spanned the length of her plaza, and four men high. She made more beasts, her personal pets, disfigured beyond the natural provisions of flesh, as if flesh were somehow mingled with fungi, stretched, strangled, and carnivorous. And she made the miserable: men whose minds she left devastated by the contents of her madness, speaking wildly, cursing the air, weeping and wailing and shouting and cowering with fear, ever to remain at either side the palace steps, striking fear in all who visited, save the Isscaran.

She wrote more books. Books that could be understood by men, which she called, the Amalgam Patheos, filled with "I am" prose, whose words were meant to be read by men as their own words. They were forced to read such things as, *"I am wretched. The filth of the earth. Unworthy of the flesh I wear. Unworthy of the eyes to gaze upon the blinding sun. Unworthy to pass beyond the woman's gate. Unworthy to enter her sanctuary and rest in the safety of soothing horizons."*

It was a slow, sour devastation. The Isscaran would hold men entangled in their arms and legs, as though children, whilst they sat in their laps, forced to read from the texts, feeling the warmth of Isscaran women, and the gradual shame of every word written in those sleeping horrors.

A shift came about. After experiencing unbearable tortures, men were cleaned up, dressed well by Isscaran handmaidens, and sent to school for indoctrination in this way, to learn the twelve wisdoms, taught by the Diamet, return home after to read a chapter from the text, and meditate on it for three hours, overseen by three Isscaran to a man. Their clothes were then carefully removed by the handmaidens and they were laid in bed, where the Isscaran took over. They would briefly massage the men to prepare them, please them a little to set them at ease, and swiftly transition to violent rape.

The Isscaran slapped them about, scratched through their skin, choked them to the point they felt they might die, and humiliated them by repeating the words of their queen's books to them, of course replacing the "I am" with "you are." The men were expected to read another chapter come nightfall and meditate on it for an hour before they slept. Always, the Isscaran slept with them. Sometimes, the Isscaran wrapped themselves around them, forcing their faces into their backsides. If they found it difficult to breathe or to sleep, because of fear, anxiety, overall discomfort or the like, a toxic fluid was ejected onto them, forcing them to sleep. Murmurs of nightmares were commonplace. The next morning, the process repeated.

Successful indoctrination was merited when men believed the words they were condemned to ingest. When they at last became what they read. This was the first transformation, beginning a return to a form of civilized society.

There was a period of rest from schooling, one month between, during which time, men would be stripped of their fine clothing and sent to endure more torture. Eventually, schooling came to be the more desired experience. The queen salivated over this during graduation ceremonies, as men exemplified how broken they were by her words. She anointed them with that loose liquor, letting it pour from her tongue as they knelt before her with open mouths, betrothed to their unworthiness. She went further to lick them passionately – a parting act of humiliation and to overstate that they, in all their frailty, belonged to her.

Those who did poorly, or exemplified repugnance toward Her Fury, were taken aside by the queen and Isscaran to experience a more selective form of torment. It started with failed men being blindfolded during transport and laid down in a room, either on the floor or on a raised surface that women could stand over, then tied to it so they could barely move a single muscle. Next, the blindfolds were replaced by the queen's face looming over theirs, surrounded by Isscaran, varying in number relative to the subject being punished, though always more than five. The queen's face was a bland stare, obscuring the appearance of intent, despite the intent felt in every aspect of the ordeal. She popped her mouth open wide and drooled on them to begin the process, simply letting saliva slip.

Her first words were of scriptures from the Amalgam Patheos, spoken in the "you are" form instead of the books' "I am." Her voice was of a soothing yet condescending melody, meant to bypass mental defenses, aided by her warm breath smelling of perfumes. The Isscaran spoke after her consecutively, all with similar tones, yet varied as a chorus and sweet smelling. The Isscaran positioned themselves all around the men's bodies so their breaths could be felt everywhere, and their words resound far and near. Lickings accompanied words as rhetoric intensified, causing rather discomforting, slime-like sensations. The feeling of lips sliding against ears as words passed beyond them. Warm breath flowing across skin.

As this went on, the queen would suddenly vomit on the men, and the Isscaran persisted the same act, vomiting whenever they felt inspired and lathering their sputum onto the body with their tongues. Sometime after the vomiting, voices once soothing and salacious, turned vicious and outrageous, transitioning from humiliation by scripture to humiliation by whatever hateful, vindictive thought came to mind. They condemned them as being foolish, foul, waste of the earth, describing in horribly vulgar fashion, the flaws of every intricate part of their bodies and of every good thing they could think of themselves. They invented anything, any unimaginable, bizarre, and incomprehensibly negative thing they could think of to tear them down.

They mangled their faces to seem as angry and monstrous as possible while they shouted with guttural wrath at the men and screamed at them. They offered haunting laughter, roaring, cackling, and screeching, mimicking the sounds of weeping that became laughter. The queen by her power, made all their faces exponentially more grotesque, distorting them with bleeding injuries, beastly eyes, morbid smiles with filthy, bloody teeth in places they would not be, and mouths stretching wide to reveal torn and separating flesh pooling with blood.

In the midst of this maelstrom of mayhem, the queen periodically turned about and spread her legs so the men could see her genital crest. Every opening brandished its own contorted, monstrous face. She slowly released heaps of the foulest smelling excrement on their faces, then sat down upon them and slid backward and forward, rubbing it in deep until they suffocated. The Isscaran gave their own offerings for the queen to blend into the mixture, as well more vomiting. The men's mouths were held open and vomit poured in with all else until they couldn't contain any more. In all, hateful speech, sounds, and monstrosities maintained, amplifying to incomprehensible extremes.

Men undergoing this process, could not help but submit to maddening sorrow, weeping and screaming in terror throughout. They were teased and goaded every time they broke. Some convulsed as their whole beings did all to reject, unable to process such horrid depths of depravity. Their bodies fought so wildly that they too released all manner of excrement and fluids from every available exit, so overcome that they simply rejected themselves in the upheaval of unimaginable hatred.

When there was no will left to fight, near complete catatonia, all went silent. Ended, as though it never was. All the waste and fluids were gone, and the men were clean. Then, and only then, for one final act of humiliation, the queen and her women aroused them with their mouths, using their tongues that were once tools of torment, now as instruments of merciful insult. They laughed and giggled, teasing the men with a soothing subtlety, stressing and slurring their words as though they were truly frail or infantile, goading their arousal with an overwhelming chorus of moans and vocal distortions.

The men often wept through this process, feeling all control sapped from them, forced to surrender to a pleasure poised to demoralize. The climax felt like the body's violent attempt at holding on to what little value was left, and the final release of fluid as the soul departing. It all ended with long, deep kisses from every woman present, last of all, the queen.

This began at the beginning of the seventh year, and before that year's end, she had hundreds of thousands of men mortified and molded this way. She was doing it; successfully rewriting Patashan, destined to spread this practice until her words became life.

CHAPTER 16

BALASHAH

I have mentioned the crater of Balashah, a place where truly all things came into perspective. All the queen is, revealed themselves to the continent on that day.

It was during her conquest, not long for the year's end, that many outlying nations and settlements joined forces to resist the rise of the red queen. They amassed an army of millions, determined to take the fight to her whilst opportune. But the air betrayed them as did their impatience, alerting the eyes and ears of Gishona in every part of the known world. Word came by wing, a Haldinian hawk, bearing the message of revolt just days after the king of Haldinia departed to meet with his cohorts.

Gishona smiled at the challenge, sending messages to have them meet her in open land at the site of the crater. A half-mile in diameter, it was widely regarded a hallowed place where the heavens were believed to have first touched the earth. The alliance agreed and the game was set. Maldresh, the coalition was called, so confident they would win. But also, desperate.

The Maldresh coalition attempted wisdom upon arrival, dispatching scouts to determine the possibility of a trap. But all they found was Gishona herself, naked, standing center of the crater fifty lexims deep, waiting, and me, a pillar of flesh by the far edge, bathing in the midday sun. The crater floor, they found, glistened as fine glass. They reported back to their commanders noting their suspicions and were ordered to engage.

As they rushed in, two staying behind, they half expected some surprise. But there was nothing. And there was no place to hide, as one could see for miles in every direction. It was when they met her that they were easily subdued and one slain by her bare hands, cut in such a way that blood poured from his body and pooled at their feet. Those who watched were shocked with fright. The other who went in to fight was held in place at the neck by the queen's right hand, his eyes beholding a face of delight as he struggled to breathe. But then the queen smashed him against the ground, snapped his limbs, and raped him with a mad smile before biting his flesh in several places, letting blood flow, and finally, his neck.

With meat in her mouth, she told the two remaining to have the whole alliance come and fight her. No tricks, no army, just her.

And so the alliance poured in, aghast at the queen's seemingly foolish decision to fight them alone. It was in this battle that Gishcna let loose all her rage and feral power. Her teeth sharpened, her jaws widened, her nails tapered at the tips, and she began slashing, lunging, biting and slicing skin, bone, and muscle as though parchment, rendering wounds that would spill the most blood, and continue bleeding. Weapons were completely useless against her, breaking upon her skin no matter where they landed. All the while, the earth never absorbed the blood. Neither was it dried by the sun. It only accumulated.

There was no holding back. The queen's rage was as continuous as a windstorm, bloodletting with every kill, filling up the crater with human remains. The more soldiers joined in, the wilder she became, her human visage seeming to slip away into pure monstrosity. They could barely see her moving but for a red blur, dripping wet with their fluids. They were devastated, if only driven by a gaining desperation to kill her for the sake of all Patashan.

Horrid, guttural cries of wrath roared from within her, disorienting all who heard. Those who couldn't take anymore did attempt to run, pushing through inbound soldiers, entrails, and red liquids to get away. Yet somehow, even scattered at the edges of the crater, no one escaped. All were pulled back in. The escapees most of all, were swallowed whole on the spot.

Alas, when it was done, when the last man fell, his neck peeling open by the grip of her teeth, the red queen, painted over in blood, reveled in her victory by eating the bounty of flesh, draining all fluids through her teeth, until all that remained was a lake of blood.

She swam in it, returning fully to her womanly form, the beast now sated. She at once levitated as though standing in shallow water, until the pool came up to her waist. She anointed herself with blood all over her body, from her belly to her face, consumed by self-idolization. She caressed every distinguishable part of her, sucked her fingers, and pleasured herself, letting her own fluids join the mixture. With her hands, she poured blood into her mouth, onto her face, and into her hair.

By the time she emerged from the crater, her army had surrounded it, holding every commander, king, and chief on their knees awaiting their queen's judgment. Gishona turned to the great pool and spoke over it. Her voice echoed through the air a deep yet sensual bellow, and the pool trembled with her tremors as she spoke, saying,

;; *Let never this bounty of blood soil. Let remain the carnage here yielded by tearing and lashing and bite. Let its screams be heard in the night. Let its pain be felt by all nearby. Never to stale. Never to drain. Never to dry.* ;;

Then holding the face of the Haldinian king and looking into his eyes with a dead stare, she said for all to hear,

;; *This place is called Balashah — my blood basin.* ;;

After her decree, Gishona flung the man into the air over the basin and held him there, her power over matter now on display. His clothes tore themselves from his body and the queen submerged him, then pulled him back into her hands. To the ground he went, the queen above him leaning in to bite. Painful screams followed as he was slowly devoured alive. At once, whilst he yet screamed, the queen licked slow where she had just bitten, savoring the taste, and said,

;; Sing to me, sweet lover, of blood spilled into my soul. Your flesh to make joy of my belly full. How I love the sounds you make as you fall. ;;

Those remaining were lifted altogether, and dipped in blood, given after to her soldiers for meal.

Following that foul day, it was on her way to the left-over kingdoms that she felt a sudden pain in her stomach. It burst into a silent explosive wave, barely visible to the eye, that spread far northeast across the ocean. The whole occurrence was a blink and hardly noticeable to anyone, even Gishona.

In but a few months more, every last kingdom and settlement fell to the Queen of Issacre. Her campaign had gone on one year since it began, now with the entire continent under her control.

CHAPTER 17

PRIMAHORICA DIVISION

CX17

I spoke of the ill fate of the Primahorica, yet the process…the process that made Isscaran, and subjected men to their torture between schooling… this, I reveal to you now. Take into account that all forms of torture I have described prior can be considered for what was used to make monsters of all, however divided the outcome.

What shall I say for seven years? It felt as many lifetimes in one. Both momentary and endless. A seven-year reign for a thousand years of trouble. I wondered if she could manipulate the arbitration of time, for young seemed to grow old in Patashan. Seven was as forty-two some days, and many more years on other days, were it worthwhile to assign it definition.

To understand the meaning of Primahorica, we must comprehend the cause of Primaviscera. To understand that, we must understand her. This telling is a journey. Go with me steadfast here.

Gishona was born to my contemporary and ally, king Jivaldi Shamua Hamheti and his wife, Farasha Mamuet Hamheti. They had four sons, Yusen, Arafti, Rujod, and Lamashadna. Farasha had many handmaidens who were to all, part of the family. This was the royal crest of Issacre, a nation which, though attuned to matters of spirit, where not by any means superstitious or bound to religious practice. Despite being aware of the gods and goddesses of Patashan, Jivaldi, much inspired by the spirit of Mal-Jin, was on the cusp of a new way of thinking.

He had dreams of a world come together in peace, though expressed apathy in doubt of its ability to be realized. That peace would be the result of shared sciences, ideals, technology, and conversation – a world benefiting from its unique and differing qualities. He thought that perhaps Mal-Jin was the beginning of this realization. Maybe, were it not for the red incursion, it would have been much sooner.

But this dire tale bears its focus in Farasha Mamuet. It should be noted, that name, Mamuet (Mam-yu-et), is an expression of the goddess Mamu (Mă-moo), life-giver and death bringer, who eases one's passing into the next life. Destruction, never by her hand comes. Mamuet was gifted to Farasha seven years prior by one of the goddess's emissaries, a priestess from the nation of Ta'amamu (Tah--ah-mam-ooh), a name also in honor of the goddess. Though their beliefs differed, the priestess felt inspired by Mamu to deliver Farasha this gift. Farasha, herself, believed that the blessings of the universe had no favored source and could emerge from any open gate. She gladly accepted the name.

The birth of Gishona was a torturous event which would ultimately mark the death of her mother, beginning with the most distressing pregnancy she had ever experienced. One to which none prior could in any way compare. The very first day, there was a spark, a strange ache in her head and slight disorientation. Some bleeding was to be expected, but from the ears and nose, as well as purple fingers – this was worrying to her family, most of all her handmaidens and midwife. Yet, early examinations by four physicians showed no signs of unusual cause.

Nevertheless, every day since then, Farasha felt gradually drained to the point that she could hardly move, requiring the aid of many handmaidens every hour of the day. She could do nothing for herself. Food eventually failed to satisfy, leading to agonizing migraines, retching, and a raging refusal to eat at all, punctuated by days of miraculous recovery to normal faculties and healthy habits. Other days involved bouts of intense pain, wherein she felt as though her entire lower torso, down to her inner thighs, was slowly peeling away and burning at once. This very strangely extended to her ears, eyes, nose, and mouth, specifically.

What started as only sensorial and localized, soon expressed itself on Farasha's skin and spread to her whole body. Her skin turned an even darker red than her natural golden-auburn complexion and started peeling away. She was so sensitive to touch that no one could get within a finger's length without her screaming. Open sores followed, accompanied by a creeping discoloration, turning her skin pale, washed excrement (diarrhea) and incontinence, hair loss, bodily secretions, and a deathly smell that forced all to cover themselves so they could somehow attempt to help her. What would have been a series of expected mood swings was replaced by constant fits of outright rage, no doubt aggravated by the pain, with loss of memory and awareness. Seizures were also an ever-present risk, with no traceable pattern.

Physicians where at a loss. There was simply no explanation for this concoction of symptoms. They had never seen any the like before. Farasha's sons could not decide how to feel or respond, ranging from emotional bankruptcy to gripping fear for their mother's life. They couldn't bear to be in her presence, constantly wrestling with feelings of obligation to stay.

Jivaldi did all to be strong for his wife, having endured four pregnancies with her. But nothing he knew was of any use at this point, leaving him in tears, then having to bear that weight while governing a kingdom. A feeling I knew well. The only redeeming miracle came in the form of yet another overnight recovery to bizarrely perfect health, allowing Farasha to do all things independent of anyone's assistance, and that much with good spirits and a wondrous smile. It was but an elating calm before the storm, giving everyone just one more day with mother, wife, and confidant.

The day Gishona emerged from the womb was a bloody siege, one which tore at the heart and punished the mind. Moreso than this, what should have been forty weeks was extended to fifty-one for reasons as unknowable as for all the queen's preceding symptoms. Farasha was near paralyzed from the waist down and in exceptional pain. She bled from every opening in her body. Everything in her felt like it was being torn apart. The screams were unlike any that anyone heard before, monstrous and as a broad knife grinding slowly into flesh without end. Everyone wept, as if they were themselves in pain. Blood spewed with every push and did not stop until the baby was free, carrying with her Farasha's last breath. This, was the first Primahorica ever enacted on a human being, and the only one which ended the life of the person subjected to it.

On this day, Jivaldi, king of Issacre, steeled himself more than on any other, having come to terms with inevitability, if only by a feeling – a knowing he could not shake. He positioned himself front and center so he could deliver the child himself, receiving his new daughter into blood-soaked arms. It was Jivaldi who cut the navel cord, cleaned her with warm, wet towels, and held her to his chest. His next thoughts were of utmost importance. His people, like his family, had no basis for the existence of gods or other such phenomena, despite the influences of other nations, so no such explanation would do. But once he made up his mind, before handing her off to be examined, he spoke the most important words ever uttered from his mouth.

"I name you, Gishona. Here is my daughter. My first and only. I do not know or understand by what power you have entered this world that your coming should be so violent, and cost the death of my wife, your mother. Nevertheless, this I vow: I will love you with all my life. What life my love has lost, now lives on in you."

Jivaldi remained troubled over the death of Farasha till his own dying day, bearing what pain he harbored in silence, and never expressing it in front of Gishona. To her, he showed all the love he promised, fighting back sorrow, and tasked his wife's closest handmaiden with giving her a mother's care. He did his best to comfort his sons, who could never look at their new sister as a welcomed edition to the family. Always, they harbored unease around her.

{{ I do not know, even now, if she ever meant for me to be so fully aware of her this way. But, the why or how, is a result of her need for control. For all that I saw and deciphered of her ruthless wrath, it was in her private moments with me that I pieced all I perceived together, whenever she pressed her body to mine. She was so determined to have me, to overtake me, to make me see her as she desired to be seen by me, that her beginning leaked into my mind fragmented, to eventually become whole. She wanted me to record the deeds of the violent queen, whereas this new tale might render her more vulnerable. I yet suspect that though it might not have been intended, had we more time than seven years, she would have told me, whether consciously or otherwise. }}

Within the first five years of her life, Gishona proved ingenious, prompting her father to order her tutelage under the guidance of the most brilliant minds in Issacre. She astounded them with her swift understanding of all fields of science, literacy, philosophy, mathematics, Patashi history, cartography, the arts, and any area of study in which she was challenged, surpassing all expectations. Ah, but when it came to matters of humanitarianism, a five-year-old Gishona made sure to appear fair in judgment, cleverly hiding nihilistic tendencies as she knew they would raise concern.

On the matter of her nihilism, one could not say that she was of an evil mind. Rather, her condition was such that she found herself aloof, at odds with the world around her. She failed to see the relevance in valuing anyone or anything that did not entertain her or increase her knowledge base. She was, in a word, bored, having no reason to care, and no one succeeded in giving her that reason. Whether she was listening to her teachers, studying crafts and literature, or analyzing her peers, Gishona was at all times absorbing information, mostly for the sake of approval.

Her education was a much-contained event. No one bothered to go beyond the limits of writ and apparatus when most things could be so easily understood, and when all required equipment could be brought to the palace if it wasn't there already. No one was available to show her the importance and meaning of love, compassion, empathy, and seeing the value of human life as an extension of all life in the world. It was of course casually expected that these qualities would naturally develop on their own.

While excelling in academic competency, she learned everything else she could from her father, and made sure that he valued her above his sons, though given her exceptional mind and early maturation, this was not difficult for her to manage. She was a master manipulator, even as a toddler, and adept at causing her brothers to either question themselves at every turn, or make them seem all the more incompetent to their father. She knew everything about them, far better than they knew themselves, and used this library of information to crippling effect.

I more intimately recall that, come the age of nine, Jivaldi took Gishona with him to all his diplomatic meetings and social visitations so she could see how things worked. He often pointed out the flaws in other leaders, whether it was their character, their laws, their intentions, or their experience. We at times discussed these things amongst one another. We found it of great import for progressive minds to stay together. Though never involved with the young lady, I carefully watched Gishona's progress from afar. Jivaldi was always considered a good man and a fair king, but Gishona only cared for what information she could consume and disregarded the nature of her father. His love for her was only marginally received when he gave her things she wanted.

{{ While I noticed many troubling obscurities in the princess, I too was much consumed with my own business, my mind too far off to consider warning my ally of what I saw. Truly, I squandered my sight then, or so I would have thought of myself at the time. But truer still, I was not ready then. This world of seeing was always ready for me. }}

Nine, became fourteen, fifteen, sixteen, seventeen, and in that time, free to explore life beyond the palace, Gishona experienced her most significant relationships in the form of three boys, and in acquaintances with children of the nobility.

Her first partner was, like her, indifferent towards the world and quite brilliant, allowing easy relation to one another in most ways. It helped that they could vent their perpetual frustrations to one another, often over things that seemed insignificant to "latent minds." Their shared ideals, such as they were, inspired them to experiment with most any curiosity, whether it was appropriate for them or not. The thrill of getting away with things they weren't supposed to was paramount to them. But this young boy soon discovered that Gishona didn't seem to know when to stop, or show remorse for going too far. Thus, after three weeks, he ended the relationship, leaving Gishona with terrible feelings of betrayal.

{{ Ah, so it begins. }}

The second partner was a budding brawler, won over by Gishona's own fighting prowess. Theirs was a prolonged union, lasting five months, which swung between obsession with one another and hatred, both finding it difficult to express their vulnerabilities with honesty. They competed for dominance, constantly trying each other's skills at manipulation. In the midst of disagreement, ardent physical intimacy was one of few things they agreed on and was their only language for conveying penitence. Then on to the game of manipulation again.

When the mind failed to gain the desired advantage, they turned to demeaning words and physical altercation to settle their squabbles. Nothing yet that would leave a mark. But before all things escalated to absolute violence, one day the boy failed to appear at their favorite meeting place. Gishona later found out that her friend had mysteriously died, again leaving her heartbroken, twice betrayed, and angry.

She exacted that anger on her already estranged brothers who feared her temper. She also broke into weeping fits and was inconsolable for months. If one were to have asked her, she might have said that she loved that boy. This is where her father started to regret giving her everything she wanted, along with many deeper things. Seeing this unspoken regret is what compelled Gishona to at least appear reasonable. She didn't want to lose favor with her gift-giver.

Not long after resuming business as usual, she found another outlet in the form of a group of young women who were similarly careless and proud of their parents' riches. As compelling as it was to befriend them, Gishona took no such interest, instead seeking ways to have them commit deplorable acts, as a form of vicariously venting her own frustrations. She started blending into casual conversations about things they imagined doing to hurt others' feelings and would inject small suggestions to nudge them in a desired direction.

Her suggestions entailed stealing, specifically items of great need, importance, or whose absence would sorely inconvenience their owners, vandalizing property, harassing with criticism to instill self-doubt, pretending to admire someone only to break them with the knowledge that it wasn't authentic and tease them, blackmailing, flashing or fondling boys against their will and coercing them to not tell for fear of blackmail, even orchestrating accidents that sometimes led to serious injury, and a litany of other fiendish fantasies, achieving them at the cost of little if any attention at all. The group loved her ideas and soon came to idolize her ingenious methods of inconspicuous scandal.

It was at the height of her sorority that she met another boy, one not so rich, but disarmingly kind, mild-mannered, and tender. His gentle ways instantly captivated Gishona with wonderous intrigue, tapping into her own potential to be gentle, which made magical their first day together. Her return home this time required her to be alone for a while in her room, not speaking to anyone unless she absolutely had to. She oddly felt as though she could for the first time in her life, breathe, and that breath needed to be savored.

{{ This is something of which I saw the spark in my own time with her, not so much for me, but a potentiality that would later be revealed in wondrous detail. }}

How brief a life had this wonder, as that night, Gishona felt a sudden plunge as though all the magic had suddenly turned to death. Inundated by recent feelings of betrayal and loss, she panicked, anxiously flashing through vivid imaginings of this boy turning on her, hurting her, leaving her, dying on her, any way that he might yet again render her distraught. This, she could not and would not allow. Fear and an agitated desire for control, drove her to be detached around this boy, repaying his compassion with beratement, by mocking him, calling him weak, foolish, fragile, and systematically draining his confidence until, in a matter of days, she drove him away.

All her negative feelings rebounded upon her four-fold in result, and she blamed him, sparking a new kind of flame to burn in her. She returned to the young women she had so deftly groomed and concocted a new, more dangerous scheme.

Together, they orchestrated the search and seizure of that boy, brought him somewhere remote, and there they berated him in unison, beat him, then doused him in hot oil and burned him alive. Gishona watched undeterred, captured by a deep satisfaction hiding even deeper pain over the act, as she yet again saw genuine love in his eyes through all his suffering. It was then she realized that what she feared, she brought on herself this time, when there was no risk of it at all. But this only hardened her need for control, as she would never admit to herself that she was wrong.

The young women laughed out loud, giggling over their achievement and made sure the boy wouldn't be found, all by Gishona's direction.

His parents searched day and night in endless distress, as he was their only child, one they considered a miracle for how kind a soul he was. But none of those who knew said anything, even as Jivaldi sent many a scouting party to find him, destined to come up empty.

From then on, Gishona strangely decided to leave her brothers alone, opting to pretend they didn't exist, rather than to amuse herself at their expense. Noticing this change drove them to pretend she didn't exist either, even when she would go out at night and come home with strange morsels of food. They knew something was gravely amiss, seeing that Gishona almost failed to hide what she was eating. But wisely, they determined to not press the issue. As they saw it, they could at last get on with their lives, and despite Gishona's former attempts, their strengths and intellectual competence once again had relevance in the eyes of their father. If it has seemed as though they were the younger brothers when in fact much older, it is because that was how Gishona saw them, and so treated them as such.

Ah, but what of the handmaiden tasked with motherhood? Ravion was her name, and she received perhaps the worst treatment of anyone. Gishona resented her, hating that anyone would dare replace what she removed. As a baby, she cried often and as loud as she could, refusing to be breast-fed, or to comply with any means of maternal consolation. She struggled time and again with her new mother, and insisted on throwing tantrums. She took to crawling early and did all to get away from her. The goal was to do anything to exhaust Ravion until she gave up. It often took the efforts of multiple handmaidens to curtail Gishona's difficult nature. Thankfully, they were there all the time, working together to nullify Gishona's belligerence with calm energies, encouragement of one another, and clever coordination.

But that resentment never went away as Gishona grew, taking on different faces and adopting more conniving contrivances. Among many new ways of causing distress was using her father's authority to coerce obedience, or attempting to get the handmaidens in serious trouble with him, which he never did fall for, as all it took was to ask a few questions to discover simple truths. Gishona even attempted to start arguments, steal from them and accuse one of conspiring against another, and doing all to cause as much mischief as possible. Still, no matter her fury, the handmaidens always had water to put out her fires and cleanup as though nothing was wrong. They were a force to be reckoned with, not caring for petty childish trifles. They had each other, experience with two of the four boys, and a well-established rapport with their father.

Jivaldi himself had also enough experience with his sons. And although this was his first girl, he understood very early on what kind of child he was dealing with and was prepared to respond with patience and calm.

The error perpetuating the problem, was an apologetic endearment that Jivaldi felt towards his daughter, urged by the vow he made at her birth. He felt compelled to pacify rather than discipline, unless or until she took things too far, at which point he was suddenly very stern with her. Perhaps the only redeeming factor was that he gave Farasha's handmaidens permission to discipline her as needed, with his full trust.

Try as they did to lovingly council Jivaldi to take up that mantle, he never could bring himself to do it, kindly pushing it aside by promising to consider their words or the like. The handmaidens saw every day the difficult position he was in, and at times felt sad that they were unable to do more, but understood that they couldn't be better fathers for him. That was something only he could do, and it had to be his choice. They washed their hands of the matter and did their best, well-aware of the potential dangers ahead.

Conveniently for Gishona, what set the nail in the coffin for Jivaldi, despite his strength, was that he never sought help for the trauma of Farasha's death. Her suffering was seared in his mind, at times making childish his emotional fortitude, corroding his dreams, and growing an infection of extended depression, intermittently alleviated by his role as king and moments of shared connection with his children. It hurt so much to think of his wife that he did all to avoid the issue, as though a tender muscle raging with pain under the least amount of pressure. Gishona understood very well the power she inhabited, and looked forward to outlasting them all.

CHAPTER 18

PRIMAHORICA INCISION

CX18

As a young adult, Gishona gained renown throughout the region for being a strong woman, sharp in mind, a skilled fighter, a wise advisor, and a passionate, dominant lover, for the few who attained the privilege. Though, never again would any such encounter resemble a wholesome affair. Those days were long gone – gone away with the flames of the last soul who truly cared for her beyond her family. She was also a woman of vision, granted a section of the city to do with as she wished, and began the construction of a grand amphitheater. The arena alone was one thousand lexims in diameter.

Along with accumulating royal accoutrements, her body transformed into a most unusual appearance for a woman of that time. Patashan was home to many women of many shapes, but Gishona's was a rare figure for someone of her stature. Most notable was her complete form, as that of an hourglass, with a strong, prominent bust, a firm and well-sculpted abdomen, fanning out into large hips. Her thighs were wide and her legs full and healthy. Her skin was golden as the sun's evening cast over the horizon and unblemished. Her lips were, as the rest of her, more pronounced, even her eyes, glowing hazel. Her hair was long, well past her shoulders, a dark-red with sun-kissed streaks, and she wore it in many braids entwined with threads of gold.

There was no part of her that was undesirable to most, and she flaunted her image in revealing dresses which fit her form perfectly. It was easy for her to gain most any kind of attention she desired. She was everyone's dream, whether to have her, or become like her.

By the age of twenty-six, she had spent years shadowing her father and governing in his place when needed, or when given the opportunity. She was perceived by many as just, capable in all matters and fair to the common citizen. Her brothers, for all their aptitude, were outshined by their sister when given the same opportunities. Even while they showed themselves to be more seasoned, Gishona pushed herself to do everything they did far better, and she always succeeded.

The handmaidens of Farasha saw the trajectory of all things and took it upon themselves long before to council Jivaldi's sons, reminding them of all their strengths, their value, and encouraged them to find their own paths in life. One of them, a relative newcomer around the time the youngest brother was born, married the eldest, and with Jivaldi's blessing and protection, left Patashan together for a life at sea.

Again betrayed by the loss of her greatest competition, Gishona attempted sabotage, but her father was several steps ahead and thwarted her every move. Still, he would neither reprimand her nor revoke the power he granted her. He wasn't simply grooming her as his replacement, he felt indebted to make it so, no matter the outcome.

{{ My ally…How I wished him peace then, and clarity. Monsters are made in the shadows of good men and women who fall ill with frail minds. But I speak of a clarity failed even in me at the time. I only knew that he was troubled when we met with the Comempri. He was never clear as to why. And I had my own kingdom to look after. }}

It was at this part in her life, Gishona realized she had overstayed her welcome. Her brothers were charting their own courses, letting go the constant battle for existence in Issacre. In a way, Gishona managed to relieve them of that burden, freeing them to look to their true passions, and ultimately doing herself a disservice. She looked forward to being their betters till it was no longer useful to her, and now those opportunities were gone. Evermore, powerful though she might have been, her father was still king, and made sure that she couldn't ruin them any longer. It was time for her to move along as well. Then again, she comforted herself by promising that she would get them eventually.

To begin her new journey, Gishona donned the attire of a traveling merchant and spent years exploring the kingdoms of the Comempri – a trial that Jivaldi hoped would serve to humanize her. I was unaware of her time in Erushad. I know now that she took extra care in my kingdom, gaining much more awareness of me than I had of her. During her tour, she immersed herself in all the mundane happenings of everyday life, discovered the most damning secrets, determined the strengths and weaknesses of her competitors, and saw how she could manipulate the innerworkings of each government by law, policy, religion, and social acclaim. But none of these were of much interest to her.

Of all she learned from the time of her youth till now, it was the way women were treated in society that yoked her attention and stoked her anger. It was not an obvious problem how women were undermined, but it was never intended to be. Societies from one kingdom to the next, had varying ways of preaching fairness for all, whilst limiting women's access to sustainable and fulfilling livelihoods. They very often weren't listened to, as it was generally assumed that men were the pillars of social order. Young boys were also taught to regard the words of their fathers over that of their mothers, and a mother's word was only heeded if the father did not object. The condition was not much different for brothers and sisters.

{{ This, even then I thought was the worst contention the Comempri held, for all that Mal-Jin taught us. It was coming together and denying divisions, that afforded us peace as once rival kings. Why would it be any less for how we govern our people? It is the one issue that most divided us, and so we left each to his own ways on this matter, while some of us favored a more unified world. }}

Yet, even in kingdoms predicated on social hierarchy, not every household was the same. Some men did not take this idea seriously, opting to treat their wives with as much respect as they expected to be given, or at least with more flexibility. Some communities disregarded the gender dichotomy altogether, favoring an everyone helps everyone approach to life, and we kings who agreed with it championed this mindset.

Gishona found these pockets of decency entertaining, a tickle to the fancy, but quickly grew bored of them. She looked upon kinder men as animals she could more easily tame, or thought that the respect and love they gave to their wives, even whilst their wives seemed quite satisfied by them, wasn't enough. Their wives should have been given more. She often imagined herself in their places, inventing ways to belittle her imaginary husbands, tempting and tempering their egos, provoking them to do more for her until she was satisfied, but never letting them know she was satisfied to keep them begging her approval.

{{ Upon seeing this portion of her life, it became clear to me that Gishona learned this way by the difference between her family and her people. It was a simple thing, an act, an imitation, for her to play a part that the people loved and so give her the impression that she *was* loved. But all that while, those who knew her closely, especially her family, were not amused and thought nothing of it. Her competitive spirit and need for control did all to drive them away, rather than force them to appreciate her presumed superiority. She further realized that even her father, despite his genuine love for her, did not approve of the woman she became.

Her soul needed to feel love, but always she desired to control the way in, forcing love to prove itself, compete for her, rather than invite it. Never does love force its way. It must have access to our vulnerability to fulfill us from the inside out. For Gishona, being vulnerable meant not being in control, and so, when all her family, save her father, retreated to the safety of their own paths, she vowed within herself to never allow anyone to know her truly. Especially not after the harsh lessons learned by her first relationships.

Nevertheless, I sense something deeper here. Surely these past attritions were not enough to erupt into the monstrosity known to me. What pain she carries has been with her since she was carried into this world. This is not to say that her wickedness is truly inherent, but to suggest my suspicion that there exists a prior, more ancient trauma which energizes her wild animosity. }}

When observing people genuinely help one another with shared respect and reverence, it all looked so wrong to her, or at least, out of place. She simply couldn't understand how people could be so good to one another in kingdoms where the powerful might question the value of their actions and rob them of their freedoms. She imagined taking that goodness away and watching their little communities crumble. What if she were to kill their little boys, abscond with their fathers in the night, murder them and steal their valuables to cause distrust, take away their food, their money, their homes? What then would become of all that kindness? Would they not fall prey to their inner weaknesses? Their darker nature?

These examples of love offered Gishona no means of sating her darker appetites, and so were of no value. It was only when she discovered untold abuses women suffered, particularly by men, having to resort to selling themselves to get by, or being sold for sport and pleasure that she felt alive with purpose. These were a people she felt she could level with, for they knew the true cruelties of human nature, as she saw it. They experienced firsthand how love, though pleasing for a moment, could not dispel the pain of having it torn apart in exchange for worse torment. But then, how could she who never gave it a proper chance know the difference?

She did at times answer this question without the asking, proudly explaining her motivations to those who would listen.

;; Once you allow the subtleties of goodness within, you can never let it go, and either you are deeply wounded by it when it is snatched from you, doomed to long for it, never to be satisfied, or if you dispose of it yourself,

you always have it in your memory, ever reminding you of what it felt like or how it could feel, then to be your finest weakness when strength is most needed. Never let such trivialities as love master you. ;;

Having had her fill of knowledge, Gishona returned to Issacre and saw to it that her father died of a terminal illness in his old age. It was one that Gishona created herself with an assortment of chemicals from various plants. On his death bed, Jivaldi declared her Queen of Issacre, bequeathing all his royal accoutrements. In a moment he privately shared with the physician who cared for him, he offered a final lamentation, saying,

"May the stars forgive me for what I have loosed upon this world, for better or worse. I thought, by chance, that I inherited one of them. It might explain the strangeness of Farasha's death. Are you a star, my Gishona?"

I call Jivaldi my ally. That is all he ever was to me. Our time together, our discussions, were always as allies consorting as decent kings do. We exchanged concerns, advice, and shared interest, as individuals who were part of a collective working in concert to realize a collective vision. Our interest in each other's well-being was a matter of ensuring the well-being of that collective...I wished, at the time, that Jivaldi had been my friend, and I his. I wished that we were closer, that we invested in one another's well-being for the sake of one another, and not only the sake of the collective. Perhaps something could have been done, I thought – some things prevented.

I understand things differently now. I know that his soul is well, and well-loved. He is with Farasha again, for a while. "Until next time, my friend."

CHAPTER 19

PRIMAHORICA ASSERTION

When Gishona emerged as queen, she appeared to the people as beautiful as she was in her younger days, an idol of presence and maturity. She wore a headdress which gave form to her hair as the mantle of a crested serpent (cobra). Her aura and appearance had such a powerful influence over any who saw her that they could not but feel unworthy, submissive, overwhelmed by a heavy, distressing sensation, goading them to crave her approval. This affect aggravated many an ego amongst the leaders of both nearby and distant kingdoms, for all who received word of her new station. Members of the Comempri were no exception.

In that same year, her amphitheater was complete, and she called it, the Primaviscera (Pre-ma-viss-era). The foremost sensation. Soon after, she began her next building project, transforming her father's fortress into a stepped ziggurat that towered over all other structures in the nation, crowning it with a new palace. This was yet another monumental effort to which she devoted ten times the manpower…and her own energy. This may be the first time she knowingly used her power. I am yet limited in discerning how her energy functions. Hers is such a strange structure of entanglements.

While she waited, Gishona called for a meeting with all kings of the Mal-Jin Comempri, and we honored her call, curious as to what the new queen would bring to the table. When we met, Gishona petitioned for her acknowledgement as a member in place of her father, a decision requiring unanimous agreement. After a full review of her accomplishments, some of us did agree, but most forthrightly declined, as she would be the first queen of any kingdom. Not only did they refuse, they scoffed and heaped insults upon the woman, stating that despite her father's dying wishes, she had to relinquish power to his eldest son, or her own if she had one, leaving a steward in place until her son came of age.

To the Comempri majority, the audacity of Gishona was perhaps the greatest offense of character anyone had ever committed in their presence. Despite arguments by the few of us who supported her, Gishona was ultimately shunned. Her anger was ready to unleash a rage most unsavory, but for her ability to assert self-control. She handled herself as any competent leader would be expected to. I wondered if somehow it would have been easier if every man approved her request. Nevertheless, she knew this would happen, and so had taken her first step. Now for the next.

Another tour she took of the Comempri, this time to gain favor with the people in secret. She appeared to each culture as one who appreciated its customs, making her a woman of every kind of people, and targeted the most needy, giving aid to those who could not help themselves — men and women, so to maintain the appearance of impartiality, which would advance her fame. She was careful to mind those who could not be trusted and used those who trusted her most as her eyes and ears where she was not present, for if any king knew what she was doing, she would surely be stopped premature to when she intended to be.

This was her campaign. One shared law throughout the Comempri was that, while the people's voices could not overrule a king's, if enough unanimity there was among them on any issue, the kings had to respond and meet their demands in some way that would satisfy. Otherwise, that king could be viewed as unfit, and should another show himself more capable, the people could demand a challenge on the other king's behalf.

While an unorthodox approach, Gishona did it justice. There were always cracks in a king's capacity to oversee his people. It was very difficult to satisfy every need, every desire, and maintain proper ordinances. Some of us were even neglectful of our people in some ways – very critical ways. What wrong could Gishona have done if she succeeded where we erred?

But then, this posed a problem. The Comempri was formed on the basis of balance between powers through collaboration. A way of keeping each other in check while ensuring peace in every kingdom, allaying the onset of war across the continent. This also meant the assurance of allied assistance where required. We were the great powers keeping other kings outside of us in check as well. What Gishona was doing was positioning herself to be the favorite of all peoples from every kingdom in the Comempri. Our neglect of women and supposed undesirables, also gave her an immense palette from which to paint herself a finer picture. Follow this equation to its end, and you see clearly the outcome. And if that, then she would be the first of her kind twice over.

Eventually, the people spoke out. Less so in kingdoms helmed by those of us with a more progressive approach to governance. There were sixteen of us. Only five governed with the people in mind. The rest found their repugnance, unearthed by a desire to assert control. They attempted to assassinate Gishona quietly, however to no avail. Gishona sent the bodies of their assassins back, bloody and scarred with her own signature mark, inflicted by her nails. She made clear that she knew exactly who sent which assailant, and that it only served to reveal who plotted against her.

{{ *This, I found to be a most extreme reaction by my contemporaries. We willingly forfeited the use of assassination and any underhanded method of control when the Comempri was formed, as it disavowed the spirit of our agreement. True that Gishona was not a member of the Comempri, yet she was nevertheless the rightful ruler of Issacre, and a fair candidate for membership. Was her request so outrageous that it* warranted a death penalty? or any penalty at all? By even attempting this, they risked wounding the validity of their own rights as kings. They were giving her all the leverage she needed. If she but uttered allegations of attempts on her life by any of us, all of us could easily be viewed as villains, or at the very least, untrustworthy. Is a king a king if he is not trusted by his kingdom? Did they forget? Or, did it not matter? Was Gishona a necessary exception? Truth, we all know better now. But we did not know then, making this act of dark magics altogether wrong. Behold, by enforcing through false undertakings the permanence of failed traditions, the Comempri kings proved the Issen queen right, and made themselves blind to their falsehoods. }}

With the bodies came a message from the queen, accepting the people's challenge and stating that if the kings wanted to claim Issacre, they must fight her for it to prove their worth and superiority in the Primaviscera. Her terms were that they engage her bare-bodied, without weapons of any kind. It was to be a fight of sheer physical aptitude. She gave her word that they may attempt to kill her, but she will not kill them.

Incensed, the majority kings agreed and the challenge was proclaimed in every kingdom in the Comempri. It was to take place after three months. In that time, Gishona did something no one would have guessed. She dwelled for a while in each kingdom, dressed in simpler, more common robes, which covered all but her eyes, and slipped into the bedrooms of each king at night. She woke them gently with soothing touches, soft, pleasant whispers in their ears, and when at last their eyes opened, they beheld her in all her nakedness. They saw who was to them the most beautiful woman they had ever seen. How they failed to recognize her, may have to do with the removal of adornments and makeup prior to meeting, and in the things she did to them, with some influence being the result of close proximity.

While their wives never once stirred, she came at them with disarming tenderness, never giving them a name to call her, but instead telling them how great they were, describing how lovely she thought their bodies to be, specifying each part in detail with gentle caresses and warm massaging. She allured them with an experience that would shame even the most blissful of passionate dreams, for they felt sensations no other woman had ever made them to feel. When she was finished, the effect was so relaxing and left them so deliriously pleased, that as she kissed them one last time, they drifted back to sleep, and she would say at last that they'd see her again.

When the kings sprung to life after their first nights, seeing that all was as they left it when they went to sleep, they questioned themselves, not able to decide whether what they experienced was real or fantasy. It felt like a memory. Their bodies knew it, still basking in the glow, and yet, though vivid, it seemed like a dream. Who was that woman? Was she an angel? Was she real, or simply the best dream they'd ever had?

Determined to know the truth, some sent patrols to learn the whereabouts of this woman. They were outfitted with modest attire, out of respect for this elusive lover. They did not want to scare her away, no matter how urgently they sought after her. However, despite their finest efforts, no one knew of the woman or saw anyone enter their palaces at night.

Certain kings decided to wait for her, choosing patience over urgency. Those who could not, either attempted to stay awake all hours to catch her in the act, or were unable to fall asleep, given their excitement, with a touch of fear. But it was not until they succumbed to weariness that they were met by their midnight mistress, awakening to her body nestled atop theirs, while others were gracefully stolen from behind and disarmed by swift and enduring kisses. They were so overtaken by the experience of her that there was never a chance to inquire of her disappearance. And as nights went on to weeks, they soon stopped caring.

Her tenderness, by then, had grown into something more possessive – even aggressive – yet mingled with so much pleasure that the kings yearned to submit to her every whim. With a soothing, silky voice, she demanded that they give themselves to her, promising that if they bent the knee to her there, she would make them and their kingdoms great, and they believed her. All but one.

There was one king, Diav Neti, a younger man to whom Gishona had nothing to prove. He was one of the progressive minority in the Comempri who supported her. I wondered why she selected him, given how she targeted those who stood against her for this ritual. But then, there was always part of her that wanted someone nice. Someone from whom she could retain a semblance of kindness, even though she anticipated pain. Afterall, she had no kindness to give herself.

Diav, despite such enchanting nightly affairs, felt himself becoming estranged from his wife, beset by a warped mind, and it left in him a bitter taste. He remembered that he loved his wife and had already given himself to her. His muscles ached to even consider letting go of what he had come to know in the night, but decided that it wasn't right, and that his wife's blindness to it all was intolerable. Thus, one fateful night, Gishona came to him and was immediately turned away. It was gracious, yet strict. Diav repaid her in gratitude, but sealed the door to any further affection. Despite all she felt, Gishona respectfully let him be. He would not even allow her one last kiss before her departure.

The next night, Diav awoke from slumber, feeling himself tied to his bed with all limbs outstretched. Seeing the bindings on his left leg, his gaze shifted to his wife's bleeding body slashed on ever part, slit neck still draining fluid, and on her face, the look of horror, staring back at her husband who could no longer console her. Devastation struck him as though a blow to the head, his mind crumbling in a torrent of tears, hollers, and dazed murmurs.

After the realization that he could struggle but not move, Gishona appeared from beneath the foot of his bed and climbed on top of him. She dominated him, painfully raped him, teased him over the death of his wife, belittled and beat him with her bare fists for refusing her, and then to spite him, gave him the most euphoric experience yet, doing all of what she did before, and much more.

She brought in help. Several women entered the room; women she found who cared little for his broken state. Women willing to take advantage of one so vulnerable. They with Gishona overwhelmed Diav, causing him to feel things he had never felt before. His body screamed. His body screamed.

She did to him what was done to me. It ended three hours after. Diav's body remained suspended in reaction, shivering, wincing, and unable to orient itself. She, they, toyed with him in this state, as though subtly provoking a wild animal.

In the nights following, having removed his wife's body, but not the blood, she held him hostage in his own house, ever bound to the bed day and night. She fed him to keep him alive, nursed his wounds, washed him, and caused him to sleep, only to wake up every night so that she could overwhelm him again. His body knew not rest. Always in the end, he felt defeated, demoralized, and broken beyond repair – forced to falsely agree to what he knowingly turned away.

What for him began as an angelic encounter, was now his torment. To seal this engagement, Gishona bound him to the foot of the bed, sitting up, his head facing her so he could look upon the gate of her oriva. Then, holding his face, she looked down on him with a possessive stare and mounted herself upon it, grinding him inside her with great force, so that he understood what he was worth to her. The rest of the kings professed their love for her, that they would forsake all others to belong to her, and she told them the same of herself.

Come the end of the third month, the masses gathered at the Primaviscera and watched as eleven kings strutted out into the midst of the arena, awaiting the arrival of the queen of Issacre. It was that morning, early, when she approached me. I was to watch the dismantling of the

Comempri from the safety of the crowd, as were the four other kings who supported Gishona from the start.

There was a moment in waiting. The eyes of the crowd from above. Their judgment descending upon the kings, emasculating their nakedness, slowly carving their confidence as though cooked meat. They were not kings anymore. They were men, preparing to be served to someone other than man.

When Gishona did appear in the arena, it was not in royal fashion, but as the lone mystery woman, cloaked in the simple robes she wore to steal their dreams at night. While the kings stood perplexed at this subtle display, she opened her robes from the chest down to reveal her body, much to their initial shock, and then her face, letting her garments slip to the ground.

The kings could not speak. Their minds scrambled to understand. In an instant, they were transported to their bedrooms, now beholding that beauty which slew them in the heart of their own homes, seeming an angel of the shadows, now made bright in the sun. Though her face did not show it, Gishona's eyes reveled in the mixed palette of fear, awe, anger over having been fooled so viciously, the bewilderment of realizing that it happened to all of them, the shame of having confessed their love to her, now suspecting that her love and all her promises to them were an imitation. Although they tried to fight their feelings towards her, their training was so effective that all the emotions of their experiences came flooding back, driving them to spill on themselves.

One last time she said to them, ;; *I did not lie to you. Give yourselves to me now and I will make you great, even the greatest of all kings in the world. I will allow you the nights you remember with me, for as long as you live. Do you not remember? You have already pledged yourselves to me…Refuse me now, and this will be all the greatness you can achieve.* ;;

She reached down, grasping a chain in her hand, and tugged at it twice. From a door afar off in the wall of the arena, limped Diav, the one king who refused her. His body was bruised and his wrists were bound together with his neck to which the chain was attached. When he was half of the way, she wrenched him to the ground and dragged him to her feet, smiling at his moans of pain from the abrasive sands, whilst never averting her gaze. Then with ease, she picked him up by his hair, held him at the neck, and presented him to the others.

After giving them a moment to observe, she threw him down on his back, crawled over him and serviced his face like a toy for her pleasure, eyeing the rest of them with menacing charm. She smothered the young man until he begged her to stop, and she paused, only to continue. She kept on until she felt herself shivering with ecstasy, until he could no longer beg, his body flailing for breath.

The men felt compelled to watch, whether they would desire it or not. From the moment they watched, they felt soiled flesh against their faces, their lungs unable to inhale or exhale – all airflow stunted. As the young man's body quaked, scrambling for recovery, so too did their bodies quake. What if your mind was stretched between? What if in seeing, you also experienced? as in a dream? The perspective of the avian and the dust? What if, in seeing another humiliated, you saw yourself?

When their mistress finally had her fill, she released the young man, and for added insult, loosed a heavy stream of fluid upon him the moment he gasped for air, causing him to choke on his first breath. As he did, so did they, brought to their hands and knees. Still compelled to enjoyment at his expense, she raised his head by his hair and smothered him again, rubbing his face in her fluids. The others followed, feeling their heads sway with the pushing and pulsing of her body.

Gishona grinned wide with wild eyes, enamored by this newfound delight, and took it further. She slinked along Diav's torso, down to his indera, and pleased him. She watched the others with eager excitement, seeing their bodies thrown back, flailing on the ground, contracting, their breaths hurried, and their eyes rolled back. She amplified the experience with moans and sighs, their noises far louder, bringing the young man to the point of release. And as he did, so too did they.

The queen of Issacre stood up over them as though having conquered beasts to their deaths. She sneered with pride as she observed them then overcome by a vision, seeing the ground beneath their bodies take the shape of what regions they governed, and saw herself ruling them all. As the men recovered, barely able to gather themselves, she said,

;; So much strength for so frail a form. You hide your feelings, your vulnerability, afraid to live in honesty for fear its precious nectar will be robbed by another. You fear the loss of what makes you man. You fear the loss of what makes you king. You fear the loss of what makes you loved. You fear. Therefore, you hide. Do you hide also from your wives?

Why? Why would you fear me? Did you not realize that by attempting to stop me, you admitted my victory? You hid behind insults and assassins, keeping warm your vulnerability from the cold night of loss. You hid from loss though you had not lost anything. What is the got of gain if you only fear to lose what is gained? And now you lose to me. I am the better of all of you. I control everything you value. You have no power without me. My tongue is the cord which binds you, all that you are, rendered appendage of my will. I am your pleasure, your pain, your pride. I am your capacity to live. I will you to rise, to fall, to bow, to prostrate before me. I will you to eat, to drink. ;;

At the word drink, she went and stood over every man's face, and urinated on them. *;; Drink! ;;* she commanded them, and whether they wished it or not, their mouths opened and she urinated again. They drank. Though their faces contorted with resistance, attempting in vain to close their mouths and turn away, they drank. Whilst their jaws locked open to receive, their throats, of their own accord, swallowed.

Impatient, she lifted each one to her oriva and pressed their mouths against it, softly commanding them, *;; Drink. ;;*

She walked back to the young king, bidding them to stand, and their bodies stood. She sat the young man up between her legs, gently running her hands through his hair, and said to the others,

;; I ask one final time. Will you choose me, or this? If you choose me, bow, right now. If you do not, you are free to challenge me. ;;

The kings were stricken with a sickness of frustration, ill with anger, horrified by humiliation, broken by self-repudiation. Some of them had not enough pride left to stand, and so bowed, crumbling into tears. Some others attempted to approach her, but Gishona had only to utter sounds and words she spoke during their nights together, and the kings felt their emotions swelter, feeling their stomachs turn, troubled by an uncanny nausea, melting their muscles so that they could not stand.

With a voice half laughing and half spiteful, Gishona asked them, *;; How does it feel, to have me inside you? Have you ever felt so unmade, that your body is not your own? ;;*

At her words, some of them vomited. Still, they fought and reached her anyway. The first and the most violent stumbled upon her, easily subdued by a leg slip he could not see, then pinned to the sand beneath her foot, all with the chain still in her hand. With all his strength, he attempted to shift her leg, but it was like a pillar of stone to his feeble hands.

Each one after him fell to her, and she only ever moved her arms to redirect their attacks, at times grabbing them by the perch of their loins. Their conditioning made her touch instantly paralyzing, siphoning strength from their muscles as though suddenly having all blood flow cut off. Each time, she wrapped the chain around them until those who fought her, seven in total, were bound together. Of the seven, she mangled six into a bowing position, leveling their backs, and the seventh, the first who still struggled to get up from beneath her, she slammed down on top of them.

This was Anapav Yeju, a man I found most disagreeable on any issue. I warned him some time ago, that a closed mind conceals the true man from his own eyes, inviting much opportunity for those seeking to claim what he leaves unattended, because he does not see. Here that danger was visited upon him, bearing down on his flesh. Even then, he struggled arm to arm with her. She enjoyed the attempt, smiling with an innocent giggle. But when she had enough, she grabbed his neck with one hand, pressed his belly with the other, and mounted him. She parted his arms while he struggled, unable to so much as nudge her, and held his neck in one hand. She looked down on him like a goddess to her worshiper and consummated her victory for all to see.

Dreading the people seeing him so vulnerable, Anapav fought to control his feelings. Gishona countered by enveloping him in the warmth of her body, cradling his head in her arms with her head resting beside his. *;; Let go,* she whispered in his ear, *It is better for you if you choose it. Worse, if I will it for you. Keep what dignity I permit you. ;;*

The man's anger was again incensed, and he refused her. She smiled, expecting his resistance, and pressing her lips to his ear, said, *;; Your muscles are the walls of my mouth, my tongue, my throat. As I speak and sound makes these walls to tremble and roll, so too does your body move in tow. My will is your will. Your flesh is my instrument of music, and I make you to flow and sing. ;;*

She breathed deep and exhaled long. Her breath became a resounding hum, an oozing ohm, accordant waves of oh, ooh, mm, and ah, and these massaged the man's muscles, teaching them to relinquish their struggle and flow with the sounds. Then the queen pushed her body against him, over and over, driving him to the point that he could not but fully let go, with sharp surges of rebounding ecstasy forcing long cries and deep moans.

In the heat of their session, Gishona turned her face to his ears and closed her eyes, enjoying the sounds of his cries. Finally, when the king at last wailed his loudest and sighed with a quiver, Gishona pressed her lips softly to his ear and whispered,

;; Am I your queen? ;;

To which he wept.

;; Yeees, I am your queen, ;; she said in return, and then kissed him long upon his lips. Again, in his ears she whispered,

;; It feels so good to hold the scepter, until it is helmed by someone you wish to control with it. Remember this moment, for this could have been your every night. But instead, this is the last time you will ever feel any affection from me. Now you will dread every night, and every night, I will take from you, feed on you, play with you, in whatever ways please me. You will not have peace, you will not have power, you will never again be satisfied. This is the rule of Queen Gishona. ;;

When she spoke her last, Gishona stood up on the man and raised her hands high into the air as a last display of victory. Her stance was of perfect balance, defying the forces which would have anyone else fall. The crowds praised her loudly, shouting down any voice that disapproved.

But she was not quite done. Something changed. Her eyes grew wide looking down on the man, her face melting to hate, spite boiling in her skin. She dropped down on him, mouth gaping large, teeth unbound, and bit into his face, taking with her his nose and parts of his cheeks, swallowing whole the lump of flesh and bony bits. She went in again, licking up the bloody chasm. As he screamed of pain, shock and fear, Gishona licked the blood on her lips with a smile, teasing her victim and reveling in his most beautiful noise. Even more rewarding was the sudden shift from cheers to fright at this most horrid sight.

She looked at me, in the crowd, watching her. A smile she offered me, so proud of what was to her the first of many achievements. With a most powerful voice, she commanded the audience to stand and bow to her, and as they did, she approached me. I was asked of my thoughts on what I observed.

;; What think you fair my fire's rank? ;;

This was the first time I had been exposed to her more far-seeing speech. Far-seeing because it was not without logic, despite what it seemed. Hers was a tongue of many worlds. Worlds I had not the mind to fathom then. But it was not without purpose. She bade me understand, testing my capacity. To her I said, *"I am grateful your mercy by matron's miracle spared the essence of your vanity."*

She giggled at my reply, cleaned blood from her belly, and gently held my head against it, brushing her fingers through my ungrayed hair. *"Come with me,"* she said, *"Come with me and hear the tones by fire and fear and blood begotten, pain crafted into kings' ransoms worth of unfettered glory and gain. Illness abides us affording many hazards for making meat dance. Dance for me, meat. Dance…Oh Patashan, my great dish. Your taste I savor most."*

Why do we do it? Men. Why do we hide our vulnerability, starving it of sustenance, denying its existence when we too, need that connection? Why do we hide? Why do we deceive ourselves, fortifying our willpower, choosing rightness over reason, might over meekness and mercy of mind? Why do we cower behind walls of pride, where others might clearly see the cracks in our foundation of lies, and rob ourselves of the power we imagined we had? Why do we betray our truth, the truth of our inner needs, for the facsimile of strength?

Outer armor may defend against the blade's edge, but it only softens the hammer's blow, suffering still the slow shattering of soft flesh as repeated thrashing ripples throughout the body like waves from a stone splashing into water. If we do not take care the softer things, then our fortifications merely delay the perils of gaining pressure, and bear us more weight to carry, until we collapse.

Seek no answer from me. For that which I know for myself is mine to know. This is a question which must be answered by the individual man. The collective can only offer a collection of individual findings for the individual to take, as fruit from trees, and try for taste. But this is a fruit of the individual soul, produced by its own journey. Connect first with your own vulnerability, and you will understand why.

CHAPTER 20

PRIMAHORICA PERVERSION

CX20

From that day, Gishona's provocative rise to power spread fear throughout every kingdom. At last, she was free, the ruthless queen, released to set aside subtle tactics and burgeon in all she was and all she sought to do. In truth, it was not for necessity that she abided Comempri customs to collect her due. Given her display of power, that much was always clear.

In the months following, she began raising her army of what she called, Isscaran, might of Issacre, her fighting women, by going into every kingdom, wooing them to her will. She called upon relations and associations she made prior, during her first tours. She reminded women of their poor status in society, how they were viewed as being less than men, how their talents were squandered by those who only sought to abuse, manipulate, and take advantage of them, and professed that men did not know their true worth and potential.

She made every effort to tap into and cultivate their hatred of men who wronged them, their desire for vengeance, and promised that if they followed her, she would bring them justice and empower them to exact retribution. Gishona the queen, would unfetter the strength and potential of women, wasting away by the will of men, and make for them a world in which women were the supreme sovereignty they were always meant to be.

But one ultimatum did Gishona give them: that to reign with her in the new world, they had to forfeit the lives they occupied, no matter how precious, and be willing to go any length she went. In her words,

;; Break now the bonds which soften the skin and widen the womb. Seal up the gates which permit worms entry to worlds of wonders hidden there within. Forfeit all that binds you to little wining babbles unfit to be called your children, and sacrifice the fat which burdens you, that which you call husband, lover, for these cannot enter the new world with us. All what was must burn for the new now, and they are meat for the feast that makes us strong. Do this, and be purified for the finest you. ;;

This meant that each woman tied to familial bonds, couldn't simply leave, but had to kill every family member in her household, and burn everything within. This was no doubt, a difficult decision for many, but all they had to do was tell Gishona of their weakness, and she would give them strength where they had none. As simple as a breath from her mouth to theirs.

There was pain in the beginning. A forced letting, as though flesh punctured and blood emptied. There was weeping. The manifestation of broken pieces shattering as if by hammer stroke, and each piece shattered again by many strokes more. Their faces squeezed and ached. Most could not stand. There was heaving and the tension of vomiting without manifesting. Only trauma. Only death. There was more weeping, a great wailing cry. A soul's agony to the heavens. And then, the turn. Coldness washing over. Hatred taking its seat on the throne, donning their crown. Finally, a kiss for the queen, their lips to hers, and the fire. Houses burned all over, tales of murderous wives and mothers surged, and no one dared stop them, for none had the right, neither the capability.

Those women who could not endure the help she offered, conflicted by love, were divided in mind and became as wild, raging animals, screaming, roaring, weeping, and physically superior to their peers, altogether making them an exceeding danger. Gishona only smiled, kissed them, and set them loose upon their cities. To those initiates shocked and concerned, she said, *;; Fear not these disquieted minds. They will find their own way to me. ;;*

Following the rite of passage, Gishona showed the women her methods, how to hunt, how to fight, how to deceive, and manipulate. She gave them all opportunities to confront the ones who hurt them, and punish them, often in the manner they were harmed. It mattered not if they were reformed to better beings; they still had to pay their price. When it happened that those ones had died prior, it was their family, or anyone related to them, which suffered the penalty. One of them was a boy, seized without warning from an orphanage and forced to endure retribution at the hands of several women, completely unaware of why he was being punished. Yet, for them, there was no other option, as he who raped them long ago was gone, and the boy, his grandson, was the only remaining family member. The rest died of illness, years before. His grandfather was his only caretaker until his own death.

Always Gishona encouraged the women to release their pain, to do all the things they might tell themselves not to, to please themselves at the expense of those who sought to tear them down. Every woman who took that next step unknowingly partook of Gishona's power, making them bolder and more unified with each subsequent show of strength. Revenge was glorious, and the sisterhood was growing.

From one Comempri kingdom to the next, Gishona fed her believers small doses of her life-force, enabling them to gradually become more like her in character, taller with thicker builds, not needing armor or clothing of any kind unless they chose it. Their bodies were their armor. They were strong beyond human capacity, fearless, ferocious, and nevertheless, the most alluring women in Patashan, after Gishona. When it was done, when Gishona finally gathered her finest out of the greater kingdoms, she let all other women alone and returned home to Issacre, to show them what her retribution looked like. It was time to settle her own house.

Her palace by then was complete, a three-hundred-lexim, square ziggurat with several levels, each slightly smaller than the one beneath, each with its own interior, external patio roof supported by decorated pillars, Issen flags, fire braziers, statues of Gishona which glorified her physique, and entrances on either side of a center stairway which only allowed access to the top level. The braziers aligned the edges of every level, sculpted in the shape of her head. The tops of each level served as walkways for the level above, and each had stairs all around it, allowing for adequate scaling.

Flanking the stairway at the ground floor, were seven brass lions on both sides, all sitting upright, with the accurately depicted face of Gishona emerging from the lions' mane. Even the torso was her own, rising out of the lower body of a lion, and her chest confidently protruding between the pillars of her own arms, descending into hands that gripped the ground with talons for fingernails. At the top, where Gishona's personal house was placed, were a series of eight-lexim pods, like open coffins, made of clay and overlaid with gold. They stood at an angle towards the top, as if a person leaning backward rather than standing straight, and faced the palace. They were sculpted to look like her own oriva. The palace as a whole covered a diameter of two hundred lexims, forty thousand square lexims, able to house the entire Isscaran army.

Her palace was the fastest ever constructed of any known structure, a seeming impossible feat. It is no mystery to me how she achieved this. Though, I wonder how much she was aware of her own ability. The palace of Issacre was the first of many marvels to come from her, and it was now ready to inhabit whatever Gishona's purpose in its construction. So, to Issacre she returned and unleashed horror.

Her arrival was heralded with joy, welcomed by a grand procession, music, dancing, and shouting. There were no chariots, no carriages. We walked to Issacre. Many miles. There was no tiring along the way. The queen's promise to me held true. I remained at all times by her side as she decreed, and as such, I was watched closely by most every eye other than hers, even as we entered the palace plaza. I must have appeared out of place. Surely. I was the only man among them.

We took fourteen days to acquaint ourselves with Her Fury's new house, and all things within. She setup a workspace for me in her chambers, with many books of empty pages waiting to be filled, scrolls, reec pens, and all else I required. It was then, in her bed, she set her passions upon me for the second time. After reviewing her estate, she stepped outside, sat upon her new throne, and initiated the new era.

Gishona began by indulging in the worship of her image. But for minor adornments of fine jewelry, she was always naked. The queen's worship required that all her people bring every son, from newborn to the age of thirteen, as sacrifices to her. Young men from fourteen to twenty-three were to be slaves for her and her soldiers. Her sacrifices were not to be burned, or slain in ceremony, but rather bound and laid in the pods I mentioned prior. The angle to which they were raised, allowed Gishona to stand over them, lean in, and devour them, bite after bite. She had additional sections set aside that she could fit in to hold infants and small boys in place. She made her victims observe its form, and then hers, realizing its likeness, so she could say to them, ;; *Look at where you lie. You know its form. It is mine…Here, I rule. Here, I eat. Here, you die in service to me. Know that the pain you suffer, is my utmost desire.* ;;

She went on for days, eating, all through the nights with no rest, enjoying in ecstasy the pain she caused, and the cries as her teeth gripped flesh and crushed bones, licking the juices that fell through. Always she saved the head for last, breathing in the pride of power she felt whenever looking upon a face frozen in torment. By her power, she preserved their lives until she ate the heart. At times, she severed the indera, dangled it in front of them, and teased them as she held it up and devoured it in small bites.

Some sacrifices were designated to be hung and have blood drained from them – vats full – so she could make wine. And as delicacies, she set aside hands for light eating when she wasn't feasting, and at times collected indera, untrained scales, as she called them, to use as meat for blood soup, or toys, and scrotums as dumplings to dip into her mouth during entertainment, or to pass the time. All this to communicate, in overwhelming fashion, that she owned the male species; that they were not even worthy enough to be anything more than tools, or food.

The time of sacrifice was one that tore peace of mind asunder for any mother and father. Many resisted, and the punishment was the death of the entire family, save the wives, yet only after parents were made to watch the rape and torture of their children. All were stripped of their clothing. Fathers, in this part, were saved for last. The queen had their wives bound up so they could neither move their limbs nor look away as their husbands were skinned before their eyes, then tied like meat to an iron bar over a fire pit, and slowly cooked, blood boiling upon fresh muscle and sinew. It was not only the fire which burned them, but when the iron bar to which they were bound was hot enough, it seared the flesh that touched it.

Their wives were made to watch until their husbands were cooked to Gishona's satisfaction, and then eaten. She often smiled at the widows while she chewed the last morsel of meat, and teased with her tongue, taking time to slowly lick and suck each bone, taunting with moans all throughout. The women felt the screams of their husbands so deeply, after the screams of their children, it was as though having many knives slowly slicing deep wounds into the flesh, drawing out of them horrid screams of their own. I know this personally, because as I felt what they felt, I saw the knives in their flesh. I too wept and wailed on the inside, consoled only by my well-being.

This cruel and lengthy display alone, broke the minds of many women. Nevertheless, as a last, frightening insult to any resister, when Gishona felt so inspired, she picked up the bones, brought them over to the woman, and dropped them in front of her. Then, she had that woman placed on her knees with her head forced upward, looking at the queen as she stood over her, holding a long, placid stare. The queen suddenly vomited all the remains of the woman's family upon her head and all over her body. Still, there was more to this parting ceremony. The queen had her stretched out, her limbs held in the arms of Isscaran soldiers, so she could lick and eat the vomited remains off her body, and then rape the woman with only her tongue, sucking her breasts, mimicking an infant child, and finally kissing her whilst licking the tears from her face as she wept.

As a parting word of warning, the queen said,

;; Resistance to me is a fantasy found in fool's milk, and must be emptied. You are woman, but I am still your queen. All will must surrender to mine, for our new world to be realized. There is no room for resistance unless I speak it. ;;

She fulfilled this warning by passionately licking the woman's face and the inside of her mouth.

In the end, the queen had the women carried back to their homes, instructing her soldiers to brutalize them from the time of their departure until their arrival. They did so. They beat them, they bit them, they scratched them, they threw them about, picked them up and threw them again. They broke limbs, dislocated them, and pulled out their hair. Once inside their homes, they were thrown into a room and left there; left to go about their lives for a time, so that the queen could see who would live with their tragedy, or be crushed by it.

Ah but they would go it alone, having their daughters from newborn to pre-toddlers withheld from them. While Gishona favored women in this agenda, there was still no room for infant care, as she was set on burning all maternal instinct in her new regime. They were put away inside the bowels of the palace with no indication of what was to become of them.

All Issacre wept and wailed during this period. Women cried out, calling the queen, "Mahakra," or "Flesh eater," and Gishona soaked it in as though cries of joy, adopting the name as a token of power. As for the Isscaran, the next step in their evolution was to have them starve themselves for three days and then join their queen in the devouring of raw human flesh, away from public eyes.

To be eaten by the Isscaran, was the new punishment for any who resisted Gishona's command, but none were to know what their penalty would be until after they were taken away to privacy. This set an unspoken precedent of fear among the people, for all they knew was that those confiscated for crimes against Gishona were never seen or heard from again. The Isscaran were at first surprised by the idea of eating human beings themselves, but that did not make them hesitant, and as soon as they took their first bites, they began to love it.

The deceptive power of Gishona's energy was not to require personal sacrifice from these women of might, but rather to alter and adapt their preferences as soon as they agreed to anything she asked them to do, removing the inhibitions of fear and reason to doubt. Of all things, the greatest motivator was to do anything they saw their queen do.

Following the trial of sacrifice, after Issacre was cleansed of all boys and infant males, Gishona had all daughters who escaped sacrifice, taken aside to stand with the Isscaran and line the tiers of her palace, so they could watch what was to transpire. That mothers and fathers were so quieted by Gishona's ferocity, enough to empty themselves of any seditious impulse, could hardly be said to have given their daughters a sense of hope in what benefit living might provide. For rather than being killed by monsters and set free from butchered innocence, they instead had to endure with them. There was no hiding this fact from innocent eyes.

What transpired beyond this point, I discuss in the chapter, Diabolic, in which men were forced to prove their worth to the queen.

CHAPTER 21

PRIMAHORICA THE PRIME HORROR

CX21

Finally, Gishona addressed all the remaining women of Issacre, young and old, having them stripped of their clothing, imbued with small doses of her life-force, and dragged away by chains tied to their ankles, enduring all the injury such a journey would render. They were taken to a network of enormous underground dungeons carved out by the ancients for purposes long lost. There, they were kept in complete darkness, where they were starved, raped, tortured, and tormented for months, only given periods of rest so their minds could break, failing to process the unending grief, the inability to see their tormentors, and the confluence of rage and helplessness, until they no longer had the will to fight what they were trained to become.

Their torment was all encompassing. The Isscaran reveled in forcing their victims to endure painless pleasures, appealing to them as would a lover, but with slimy, tender, salacious speech, holding them endearingly, massaging every inch of their bodies, developing into four or more of them lathering them in saliva, engorging themselves with smothering kisses upon unwilling mouths, and stimulating their genitals with their tongues, coercing intense and undesired sensations which left them catatonic when it was done. After that, was darkness, left alone so they could drown in their new reality. And the process repeated. No appropriate age was spared this horror, and more delight was had when thrust upon virgins or those too young to have had any experience while in relative safe conditions.

When their victims grew cold and comatose to that priming phase of torture, the Isscaran moved shockingly into complete deconstruction of sexual organs and appendages. Whether it was their hands with sharp nails on their fingers, red-hot rods of metal, long shards of crystal glass, knives, metal clamps, wooden poles, diseased beasts, or long bodied insects groomed by Gishona with piercing mandibles, women were violently ripped apart from the outside and inside.

Breasts were torn off, shredded, pinched, punctured, bitten, and chewed. Throats were filled and forced to gag until widened, swollen, sore, and bleeding. The Isscaran enjoyed biting off parts themselves and making it as painful and enduring as possible, forcing it to last weeks.

The women of Issacre suffered brutal gang beatings until bloody and unrecognizable, burning all over their bodies, hair pulling, having their arms, legs, noses, ears, teeth, and tongues ripped off by bare hands or by apparatus designed for the task, and were often abruptly violated exactly as they were at the start.

Brutality and sensuality were used as the prime method of reconfiguring their thoughts to have no slight of hope in any kind of relief. It did not matter what was broken. Such extreme and horrid measures of deconstruction could be utilized because by the power of Gishona, all things would simply return to their natural state, all damage undone, leaving all the memories of torment present in the mind, such that the body felt everything as though recently wounded.

With every stage of recovery came a stronger body, able to withstand greater levels of pain and psychological perversion. A next-phase torture method was for the Isscaran to systematically break their bones and pull them out of sockets, effectively stretching the skin and making the women as dolls filled with sand, then to be left alone for their bodies to recover. Each time, those who began as children, rapidly aged to youthful maturity.

At each point, from the very beginning, there was yet another enduring element. Voices in the dark whispered and screamed words of hatred and accusation, goading the women of Issacre to give in to their darker tendencies, convincing them that they were monsters inside, and that to submit to it was the only path to power. At times, the Isscaran gathered around them in groups of seven to twenty, invading their thoughts with virulent voices of hate, turning them against everything they knew and everything they loved. They were fed human flesh when they were hungry enough, the first victims being the infant girls and pre-toddlers taken away during the time of sacrifice. They were also given blood to drink, retained heightened senses, and were able to see clearly in the dark.

To test the effectiveness of their indoctrination, the Isscaran brought male prisoners from other kingdoms to give their inductees someone to focus their hatred on, and ultimately convince them of disdain for the male portion of humanity. They goaded them to fear, persuading them to see men as vile and unworthy of them, to see them as this horrid thing that has no right to life or substance except to be food or to serve the will of their female superiors. When fear turned to paranoia, and then to anger, and finally to primal rage, the women of Issacre attacked and ate their prisoners, robbing their bones of any vestige of flesh.

From time to time, Isscaran would rush in, unannounced for a rapid beating session, looking forward to the day that their initiates would turn their own violence against them, proving their progressing strength of body and will.

The more of their humanity they lost, the more of Gishona they gained. They grew into beautiful monsters who cared for nothing and no one except Gishona and each other. It was not until they were strong enough to break their bindings that they were released and welcomed into the sisterhood.

When at last the Isscaran were complete, and Issacre was set in order, Gishona declared,

;; Until we rule together in the new world, every woman must be purified by suffering, to break the spirit of kindness, compassion, and good will, so to emerge the strongest warriors on earth. Let love be ravaged, peace emasculated, and let my lovely horrors eradicate all sense of individuality beyond what is me. ;;

Following this decree, Gishona and her army of Isscaran, now over six million strong, toured the kingdoms of Patashan, cleansing all peoples in blood and torment, as was done in Issacre, until the entire continent fell to the rule of the Issen Queen. Large dungeons were constructed beneath the grounds of the royal houses in every kingdom. This time however, men were not as fortunate as those of Issacre. Gishona had her male horde and needed no other. She could after all, create more if she wanted. This time, men were to undergo the same torment as women, to systematically emasculate them, break them, and forever hold them prisoners in their broken state.

Though indeed all methods of torment were equally reaped upon men as it was for women, some variation was implemented. To start, large fire braziers illuminated the rooms where men were kept. The Isscaran wanted them to see what was being done to them and who was doing it. And instead of the Isscaran assaulting their ears with hateful words to inspire hatred of others, this effort was directed towards persuading them to hate themselves. When they were beaten by a brood of Isscaran, it was not until every muscle within their skin was the consistency of clay. They were also scratched by sharp nails and repeatedly bitten until they were fractions of themselves.

As part of their psychological devastation, the Isscaran relished in urinating on them with their faces stuffed inside their oriva, and then grinding their faces in it. They surrounded their male subjects in groups, stood over them with their rears exposed above their heads, layered them with excrement, then sat upon them to once again rub it in. They were also made to eat and drink excrement, vomit, saliva, and any other bodily excretion the Isscaran had to give.

Men were choked, gagged, and smothered. The Isscaran bound protruding apparatus to their waists, crowned by curved blades, held men's faces and stabbed them repeatedly. The same was done in the position of intercourse, shredding their lower body, and all contained therein. Men were of course, given a portion of Gishona's energy so they would never die from sickness or injury, and always they regained what they lost.

There were seeming moments of relief from trauma. After being left to themselves for a time to recover and contemplate their new existence, the Isscaran would come to them quietly, lasciviously, tenderly, lay them down and pleasure them for a brief period, attending to every part of their bodies to make them feel as relaxed and as relieved as possible. Sometimes it was just one of the Isscaran and other times groups of them, each periodically joining in to build to a rapturous upheaval. By the end, men felt so good they could hardly process where they were, and nearly forgot the pain they endured. That was when it all unraveled into a ravenous frenzy of eating, beating, scratching, and raping, turning absolute pleasure to overwhelming horror.

The screams from both male and female subjugates, were as the soul tearing cries of children. All were reduced to an infantile state with eyes squeezed shut and mouths torn open by utterances of anger, abandonment, deep sorrow, and the feeling of powerlessness. They were barely able to speak coherently, except for an often mangled repetitious outcry of "No!" All else was weeping and wailing. And while they were left to scream during recovery, the Isscaran were so aroused by the frequency that they gathered in multitudes and pleased each other, their bodies entangled in wild passions, celebrating their accomplishments. They added their own screams of ecstasy in contrast to the guttural chorus of grief. At times, the queen joined them.

Every act of torture ever utilized by the Isscaran was first modeled to them by Gishona through many days of rigorous training, though the rigor was less the effort of the queen and more so the vigor of the Isscaran to employ what methods they were shown. Training was therefore mostly easy and enjoyable.

& & &

I once heard an elder say to me, *"The bones, the bones, I speak of the bones. The throne which sits atop a mound of bones."*

There was such a seat in yet another hall of horrors. Gishona acquired many dead throughout her endless onslaught of death, forcing men to cart and carry them from whatever kingdom to her dungeons beneath the palace in Issacre where, in a special room, she ordered them to craft a pile of bones, held together by mortar and doused in gallons of blood, complete with a throne of bones and steps descending from it. Remains decorated either side of the floor, leaving vacant a central pathway. Six tall sconces made mostly of ribcages flanked the mound in rows of two, cascading from the throne to the bottom step. Just before the first step, with a diameter of ten lexims, was a hexagonal pool of blood rising a little above Gishona's waist, so that she could baptize herself in it each time she went to take her seat on the throne. Those who approached her had to do the same.

There in that room, Gishona had the very slaves who built the throne, and any such prisoners, surrender themselves entirely to her will. There were moments of audacity, in which some who were not familiar with Gishona's strength, thought they might be able to overcome her with superior numbers. Every such provocation was quickly devoured by the bloody queen.

In their surrender, these prisoners were subjected to a maelstrom frenzy of murderous fury for the queen's enjoyment, the result of which was bodies ground to such extremes that they became as paste. Gishona both rubbed herself in their ground flesh and made sculptures with them. Otherwise, when she desired time to herself to contemplate worse deeds, she sat on her throne, awed by the knowledge that every bone beneath her was one she conquered – every individual bone. This thought process was marked by a femur which she took a moment to hold in her hand and observe.

One might wonder what political affairs and the overall governance of the peoples would look like under her rule. What would be the manner of law, order, and the dissemination of justice? For Patashan during this time, it seemed such ideas were far from Gishona's concerns. Primahorica, was law and order, to be swiftly and justly disseminated until its entire population, and soon the world, was transformed by a Gishonian era manifestation of destiny.

& & &

Over the course of her conquest, Gishona adopted a new, twisted and sophisticated horror to celebrate the conquering of a kingdom. She began this occasion by taking a selection of men, especially those in power who were most cruel to women, and having them first stripped of all attire. Next, they were laid on long tables, face-up in full view of crowds, with loved ones front and center. ;; *Be still, loving flesh of mine, ordained for teeth and wine. ;;* she said to them. By this, their bodies became still, though feeling and sensations remained.

She brandished carving knives, forks, paring knives, spoons, cups, and plates, neatly set beside her human subjects. Then with carving knife in hand, she went on to gracefully slice men open from sternum to waistline, carefully peeling back the skin to reveal ripe red muscle tissue. She allowed excess blood drip and fall where it would. From there, she carved their flesh as though a cooked boar, sat down, and formally dined on red meat, organs, arteries, and all else, reveling in the slow excruciation of her still living food. For drink, she squeezed highly saturated organs into cups.

She also gloried in the palpable aghast of the crowd, whilst some felt a growing sense of pride if they were victims of harm or discrimination enacted by the men eaten, seeing their justice fulfilled. This was a practice in which Gishona encouraged her Isscaran to participate.

& & &

In the golden era of Primahorica, whilst watching their initiates suffer, again, there was that question stirring deep in the minds of all Isscaran which began with the queen before the emergence of the monster: why were they spared the horrors they now inflict on their future sisters? They did not require being tortured to gain what they had; it was gifted to them. So why not simply offer the same to all other women? Why indeed.

Some reasoning was apparent. In the beginning, Gishona wanted to prove herself to the Comempri kings, circumvent them, and shame them. The empowerment of women was therefore much more effective and inspiring. She also enjoyed the ability to live vicariously through hundreds of women taking power from those who suppressed them. There was pride to be gained in knowing that she led them to supremacy. But the notion of deeper, more obscure motivations haunted them. So, the question yet lingered.

You see, with that question came a feeling – one of disenchantment upon the realization of atrocities committed against their own. Although they took pride in who they were and what they did, it still seemed gravely unfair to treat so horridly those intended to be their equals. Moments of reticence resonated throughout the Isscaran horde, sparked by a subtle sensation of, "This isn't right." Nevertheless, far be it from them to question their queen. The Primahorica was notably successful. Clearly, Gishona knew what she was doing.

Moments such as those were markers for droplets of pain, puddling little by little, each time the Isscaran noticed Gishona's inconsistencies, whether subtle or glaring, since the start of it all. Pain is energy. Energy does not go away. It builds and or translates into some other form of energy, as it is given a path to follow. If pain is ignored, as with other energies, it builds in an unresolved state, becoming a malignant boil, set to rupture when pierced or pushed by just the right catalyst.

All the Isscaran knew to do was ignore their pain and let it build. This is what gave them the strength and tenacity to commit any abhorrence. And they had plenty of targets on which to assert that energy. Gishona herself, was one to prefer that her inconsistencies instilled more pain. But of course, a process of this kind often reaps detriment upon he or she who sews the seed. All energy must be released at some point.

CHAPTER 22

MORE TO IT

CX22

Here, I list some other of Gishona's deeds, furthering her treatment of male subjugates. It started shortly after their first trials in Issacre. Men were divided up to serve whatever purpose the queen assigned them.

Beginning with the men who worshiped Gishona, whether out of love, obsession, or for the freedom to release their inner monster, they enjoyed all that Gishona and her soldiers did to them, even encouraging it. If it was than any of them seemed to falter in their enjoyment, the queen empowered them to enjoy it more. Yet for many others, submission was a matter of survival. The queen and her company accepted all such motivations, though there was no deception unclear to their eyes.

To all those men who emerged from Gishona's trials, was given the right to be counted among the ranks of the Isscaran, whether they chose it or not, and were possessed of Gishona's energy, allowing them to become strong like their female counterparts. But they were not viewed as equal to them. These men were to be the purest exceptions, as not many more would be granted such prestige.

All this time, men who were not fathers waited in fear, not knowing what horrors would be theirs. When their time came, Gishona once again split them up into separate groups. A large group was set apart to have their blood drained into Gishona's bath, a twenty by twenty lexim tub, much like a small pool, so that she could swim in it. That blood was infused with her energy so that it would never spoil. Another group served as her devout worshipers, consecrated to speak loud praises of the queen and debase themselves before her. They were therefore not to be harmed a great deal.

The rest were cursed by her power to never die, even if dismembered, yet always able to feel pain. They also could not speak but for making noises void of discernable language. They were divided up to serve as workers, training apparatus for the Isscaran, teaching subjects, cushions and pillows, toys, toiletry, punching sacks, and any other fleeting itch the women of Gishona needed scratched.

Gishona in particular, had a rather nasty temper ready to erupt at any moment, and exacted it upon a male slave by tying him to a post in her room and slicing his face to ground meat with her nails, or hoisting him high enough to be at eye-level with his torso, so she could slash it until she bored out a bloody crater of exposed bones and organs. She wasn't satisfied with a single scratch unless it tore small sums of flesh. She would vigorously rub her face in the exposed area and scream into it. Sometimes the vibrations of her voice ruptured the body, causing parts of it or all of it to explode, relative to the intensity of the scream.

{:} {:} {:} {:} {:}

It was whilst men brought their sacrifices to the queen after the trials, that she selected fifty of them to be grouped into bed chambers inside the palace and undergo special preparation. Once gathered, the Isscaran cut off their legs at the hip – legs and arms at the shoulders for some. They heated iron discs until red-hot and cauterized the wounds, immune to the heat themselves. Now immobile, the men were harnessed and hung, with arms outstretched for those who had arms, on a system of chains which allowed for them to be moved around the room while suspended, and lowered when desired. From then on, they were tended to daily by handmaidens to ensure the best of health, left to wait and wonder what purpose the bloody queen could have for them.

They eventually learned their purpose when Gishona came in unannounced, laid them on a bed or upright on a post, and proceeded to pleasure herself upon them until she was satisfied. Her attitude was quite a bit different here. At times, when entering any of these rooms, she did so driven by an ardent desire, a desperate urge as if demanded by something in her being, something that perhaps she could not control. It was as though she was unaware of her surroundings, relying on familiarity and instinct to direct her movements. Mating, therein, was violent and enduring, though without any act of injury. It was all a matter of what they could give, and what she needed to take. If her need superseded anyone's ability to give, she would simply move on to another. Nevertheless, they had to give.

Yet, even when Gishona came in to them with all her faculties intact, she still offered an unusually tender, pleasant, and perhaps, frighteningly silent approach, entering with a placid expression, fully expecting that they understood they were not allowed to speak unless she ordained it. She went on to indulge herself with the appearance of kindness towards them, as if they were her lovers, bathing them in her flesh in any way she felt to do, all while they laid or hung completely surrendered to her desire, whether they desired it or not.

Her lips, teeth, and tongue spared no part of them, digging in impassioned with slithering motions and subtle moans, as though enjoying a meal. She favored lowering them to the floor so she could grind their faces, reminiscing the accomplishment she felt when she did the same to a subdued king for the first time. But that was all. These dangling bodies were otherwise barely acknowledged, rarely ever looked in the eyes. She simply strolled in, grabbed them wherever, however, and did her bidding as though some past-time pleasure. The men were nothing more than exercise apparatus, toys, dolls…things.

If Gishona felt inclined to more than customary, she invited several of her Isscaran to enjoy these more graceful occasions with her. A man in this wise was smothered by passions and sensations he might have chosen to experience under more favorable conditions, even idealizing a life of love and happiness if that was his bent. But instead, he was there to be occupied at the behest of beautiful strangers who touched, tickled, nibbled and slurped, lathering him with loose fluids while talking amongst themselves, pleasing themselves and each other as if he were lifeless – a husk to be humped, helmed, hassled, and left alone until they felt inspired to do it again.

And what should any of it have mattered to these leftovers? They were perhaps the most fortunate of those with a lesser lease on life – by Gishona's standards. With the exception of missing limbs, they were treated well. They were regularly fed and watered, the food was good and the water clean, they were strong and healthy, no risk of injury, illness, or death. Despite a slight of minimal boredom, all was fair. Even being hung offered no strain on their bodies whatsoever, given the careful craftsmanship of each harness. Having fluids washed down their throats might have been a minor annoyance. Nevertheless, they were clearly not designated for pain.

But then, after the initial dread of wonder at the possibility of horror passed, there came in its stead the wonder of an experience with someone they wished they could call a lover, only to have a feeling creep upon their minds as though slowly submerging beneath still waters. A feeling that this entity waxing their bodies in outpourings of erotic ritual, cared nothing for the mind inside the skull she held and kissed, had no need to nourish the eyes with glances of love and longing, and no will to wash over the ears with words that reassured lovely knowings already felt and understood. Of course, no such fantasies could one expect to be realized in Gishona, and they knew it. But to bask in the withdrawal of being so close to a vision of fairer findings and yet so far from tangible form, was where their torment made its bed.

{:} {:} {:} {:} {:}

There was another notable event. A time when Gishona secretly settled in sabbatical for a month's duration, while she gave birth to between thirty and forty children a day, amounting to nearly a thousand when she was complete. It was at last discovered that she had withheld gestation since conception and accelerated it at will when she was finally ready. For her, this most unnatural process was painless and her offspring, mostly girls and some boys, emerged roughly every twenty minutes in succession, to be handed off to women charged with raising them in her ways. They were due for a difficult life.

No child was more precious to Gishona than those formed in her womb. Male offspring were for once, no exception, and it was at first unclear as to why. This was something I understood, the answers rendered clear. While I am not yet equipped to speak on the logic or the lack thereof in her decisions, there is a matter of control here which motivates her. She made these children herself. They came from her body. They are her creation. They are tangible iterations of her sovereignty. The essence of her new world, having no blemish of the old world. All are pure and all are hers. Therefore, all are equally valued.

These children were sent away with their assigned mothers overseas, to spread to every part of the earth before her own eventual emergence, as only she presumed she would. Following Gishona's off-sprung diaspora, the men whose torso's she reduced to vessels of pleasure, save some, were carefully carved on platters and slowly eaten alive. It was as much a thank you as they were ever going to receive. Their mealtime horror, long thought to have been evaded, finally came due.

{:} {:} {:} {:} {:}

The night I was laid to rest by that womanly being clothed in light, my friend, was the night I witnessed a face I had not seen before from Her Fury. A name does come to me now, one I may call my friend – Shi-han, Shi-han.

In anger, the queen hid herself in darkness and did not sleep. Her chambers were so dark that almost nothing was visible, despite the moon's light. She watched me with glowing eyes from the upper left corner of the room – a looming stalker. After a few moments, my eyes brightened, allowing me to see clearly in the dark. She was suspended there in that corner, seated between her knees, her hands grasping the wall beneath her as though a statue. She had a stoic grimace about her. All was still except her eyes, following my every motion. I inspired more bitterness in her because I could see her beyond the darkness. And it rendered bitter reprisal.

She spent two weeks of nights on the prowl, terrorizing men and children all throughout Patashan. She did little physical harm beyond biting and clawing…it was the fear she wanted. She desired to experience raw fear. She would startle them, cause them to wonder if danger lurked in the dark, appear and vanish to breed uncertainty, and make strange sounds to disorient. She would pin them down as they slept, rousing them to find they could not move, while a monstrous face gazed upon them with sharpened teeth and an open mouth dripping with blood. She would do anything to make them uneasy in that state, assaulting them with disquieting sensations before vanishing suddenly, leaving them to wonder when the next encounter would be.

Her victims would sometimes sleep only to wake up with cuts and sores on their skin that seemed to come alive. Sometimes it was waking with a feeling of choking. Sometimes she spoke frightening words of hatred. She infected their dreams with wild nightmares, causing many to scream themselves awake. The difference between the dream and reality was indistinguishable. So many things she did. So many things. She trained them to fear her, so much so that they muttered to themselves, paralyzed by fear. They could not look at her, eager to run away at the slightest glance.

In all that time, she did not so much as acknowledge me during the day, except to award me sneering glances, making sure I was doing my part. She otherwise seemed her proud, boastful, violent self, reveling in her dreadful deeds. But when it appeared she had her fill, come the end of those two weeks, she stumbled into her chambers one night as though drunk, or exhausted, and fell into her bed while I sat at my table. As the sun rose, she accosted me with a kiss, cheerful, impassioned. She took me away from my work and threw me onto the bed for a session.

I asked if she had forgiven me my offense and she smiled and asked, ;; *When have you ever offended me?* ;; She kept going after that. She was a child, having her fun, completely unaware of anything which came before. She at one point kissed me repeatedly and begged me to stay, promising that she loved me, over and over again. Who was this? She was delighted, excited. She lay beside me when she was done and discussed her plans with me, all the horrors she intended for the day. She might as well have been planning festivities.

That morning, in such high spirits, she selected a few of the little boys she horrified in the night, whom she arranged to be carried to Issacre while she slept, and joyfully whipped the flesh from their bodies until they were nothing more than heaps of bleeding meat. In every swing was the stroke of wrath showing itself for what it truly was. All her anger. Everything in me wept. Everything. And she…she saw that in me and raced over with kisses and hushes, telling me all was well.

She kept them alive for a time, some of them, so she could watch them crawl and bleed, listen to them whine and weep and wail and scream while she cheered! She ate them after, and offered me a piece, dripping red. I could not but back away. She seemed perplexed at first, but then shrugged and ate it herself, humming a jovial melody. Even the Isscaran found it odd. But what did they care; it served them as well as they served her.

{:} {:} {:} {:} {:}

There were days set aside for the training of her worshiping men to observe horrifying displays – to take in the sight, sounds, and visceral devastation, as an act of total surrender to her will. They gathered on the third level, on their knees around an altar, looking up at the queen.

On one of these sacred days, the queen selected a man to lie stomach-down upon the altar. His hands and forearms were bolted to its sides by nail and hammer, as were his legs. The queen cut open the skin of his back by a fingernail and peeled each flap to his left and right side. With his inner musculature exposed, she took her time prying up each rib bone until it snapped off his spine, subtly laughing to herself as he moaned and hollered. Each bone she separated, she slowly dug into his thighs and arms.

Following the cut, Her Fury gazed with dazzled eyes and a loving smile at the meat arrayed before her. It was now that she let black smog flow from her mouth, imbuing her subdued with sustaining energy to stagnate death and exhaustion from too much pain. Blood was already flowing from the tearing of his ribcage. Joy flowed next, as she plunged her hands into the meat with firm grip, opening her fingers and closing them again like chewing jaws, reducing all within to red sludge.

Pleasure oozed from her pores in the form of moisture, as it did from her eyes rolling upward and her tongue restless between her lips. She stopped briefly to snatch the face of one of her worshipers and release a violent outpouring upon his head, whilst she offered a scream to the air. Her body shook and struggled, overtaken by raging forces.

In the anointing of this unleashed passion, she returned to the altar, wildly alive, and dug her face inside the open bowl of her subjugate. She slurped, chewed, and swallowed on either side of the spine from its base to the shoulder plains. The man was in so much pain, he could only shake and struggle, his eyes bleak with shock and his mouth stretched wide to its limit. No sound there was to relieve him.

When the bowl was near empty, the queen lifted her head, licking the remains from her lips and wiping them from her face to suck from her hands. One last ritual rite, she tore the head from the body with the spine intact, and with meat still attached, dripping blood. She held it out for all to see, then held it up and fed the spine into her throat, even extending her jaws as the serpent to swallow the head whole. When her lips closed around that face, frozen in horror, she squeezed the muscles of her face and neck repeatedly, crushing all within.

As this fractured soul descended into her stomach, his last cries echoed through her skin, and again inspired another outpouring which she showered upon her worshipers. When it was done, all of them, through frailty of mind and eyes bleeding water, worshiped her, saying, *"Our queen most beloved of all! Let your beauty, your power, never waver, never wilt, never empty! Let your glory flow unceasing and our weakness please you always! Forever the Red Queen! Forever!"*

{:} {:} {:} {:} {:}

The queen had many ways to play, as an infant muddling food. But there was one way which became most special to her – something private. Privacy here was a matter of personal taste, rather than an effort to hide. She would take a man to a dark room, blind to all things conscious. He would awaken to the queen sitting before him at a brief distance, her stare bland and menacing with dull eyes. He would see the darkness around her, and notice red light strangely directed over them, making her the center of his attention. Then, he would feel himself bound as if by chains, yet not. His body was compelled to sit upward with his arms at his side and his legs partially bent outward, only able to move his head and neck.

The queen sat still for a time, staring at him. The pupils of her eyes would slowly fade into the yellow glow of her corneas, themselves gaining bright orange. The man's gaze would be locked, compelled to see her, unable to blink. When she was ready, she let her mouth peel open, wide, and out of that dark orifice, a tongue would peek, dabbling along the lower lip as though a worm finding its way in the soil. It would then slither out over the lip and descend like a serpent to the floor, steadily making its way to the man. Halfway along its path, it would increase a little in mass until two more split from either side into separate branches, continuing their approach. The splitting would repeat, until multiple branches of the queen's tongue began to creep upon the man, enveloping him.

The central tongue would travel up the center of the man as he dreaded every moment passing. Never could he look away from the queen. His body would loosen, allowing him to squirm at the ill-fated sensations of warm, slimy, slithering things sliding along his flesh. The central tongue would climb slow, encouraging a series of irritating tingles as it made its way to the neck, and then the face, such as a trickle of water sliding along the skin. The man would be unable to resist the urge to wince and move his head, attempting to avoid its approach.

Branches like vines would gather at his face, inserting themselves into his ears and nostrils, while the central tongue playfully lathered his face with saturating lashes. All the while, the queen would make a long, perpetual Ah sound, which varied in timbre and vibration. As she played with her subject's face, she might have laughed with a distorted, guttural depth, enjoying the subtleties of the man's discomfort. She was especially fond of how he was forced to open his mouth for lack of nostrils to breathe, but then attempt to resist her tongue meandering along his lips.

After play, the central tongue would recede and coil about his neck, then altogether enter his mouth, maintaining its course until it reached the stomach. Inevitably, the man would be compelled to gag, but unable.

Whilst this torture played out above, other branches would gather around his pelvis, squirming about all things between his thighs. In doing so, the queen coerced adverse and extreme sensations to work against one another within the man. He wanted to scream, but could not. He always gagged, but could not repel the cause. His lower body demanded release from stimulation, but his mind could not contend with the troubling injury of plugged ears, nostrils, a plugged throat, esophagus, and stomach.

As the man suffered, horridly so, he would watch the queen and her monstrous act for a time, before two tongue branches ate their way through his eyes and slithered out of their orbis, completely filling the cavities. The man's body would tremble, as it knew not what to do.

Eventually, the queen would release and let her subject recover – a most painful and violent recovery. When possible, there were some who would ask her why she did what she did, and her response was always the same.

;; You are mine. To do with, what I please. Every part of you. And I remind you of this for all of the life I allow you to live. ;;

{:} {:} {:} {:} {:}

Five months into her fourth year, the queen requested a portion of her most devoted women, at least one hundred in every city of every kingdom, to be given to the task of horrification. This task required that they allowed themselves to have their skin cut off to reveal the flesh beneath, to be slashed by the queen's nails and by the Isscaran, or to have a third of their flesh torn from bone and made to look and smell rotten. Most of them were bathed in blood. Throughout this process, the queen imbued them with her energy so they would not feel pain, so their injuries and external forces would not weaken them, and so the blood pouring off them remained unspoiled.

Their instruction was to lay on the ground in designated pits outside on the palace grounds, where select men were dropped in, so they could appear to come alive and frighten them, seduce them, and rape them. The women were to make the rape a pleasurable experience, all the while debasing their male subjects, teasing them, and convincing them that they enjoyed cavorting with the dead, when they clearly did not. Pleasure was often challenged by a struggle, as the men did all to break away. But their strength was meager by comparison. They would not be released until they surrendered to the women, and would neither receive food until then. They were only given water.

{:} {:} {:} {:} {:}

There is a room of dark light, a sickly green and brown glow, where the entertaining of death persisted. In this great room, where the limits of walls and ceiling height evaporated into the absence of light, piles of unliving corpses sustained in all stages of decay covered the floor. They rose to between three and eight lexims high.

At any point, when she desired, Her Fury descended into this room by a long stair, lost in yet another strangely depressed state, until she let herself fall into the pile of bodies which met her at the bottom. There within, she waxed poetic with ardent expressions of desire, making love to the dead as though living, as if themselves capable of love. She licked and caressed bone and soured sinew, swam in waters of flesh, popping in and out, and suckled rotting fluids.

She was frail here. More frail than I'd ever witnessed. More frail than made sense for one such as her. She trembled and huddled into herself at times. Even her voice was as a frightened child, mournful, dependent, broken. She asked the dead to permit her to please herself at their expense.

A moment occurred wherein she took to a man recently deceased and breathed into him. He awakened fearful and disoriented and she attempted to comfort him with hasty hands and shushing whispers. In her own words:

;; Peace, please! You are dead, my love. You are dead. And I longed to see you again. I missed you, my love. I missed you, and I long to have you with me. I brought you back; please don't be afraid. Be with me here forever. I'll bring you everlasting joy and you'll never leave me again. I'll never leave you alone again. I'll never leave you. I'll never. Please stay. Stay and make love to me. Stay and live. Please forgive. Please forgive me. Please forgive. ;;

She forced this man through his screams to mate with her, even as she was profuse in apology.

Most obscure, she would at times, sit and stare off into the dark above her, and make strange gestures with her arms and body, as if to appeal to something beyond. Finally, a sudden, piercing scream, the war horn of suffering. Do you know what this is?

{:} {:} {:} {:} {:}

The queen made it her business to gather all livestock, save some for the families she left to maintain civilian populace. Not just livestock, but various types of creatures, large and small, from across the continent, sequestering them away in her palace for a Primahorica of their own. She had plans to transform the animal world – to redefine what would be the creatures of her world. She made so many monsters, through constant torture and experimentation. She used them sparingly during Primahorica, intent on revealing the fruits of her labor only after all of Patashan was reformed. She planned also to interbreed humanity with her creations. I see now that she has completed her experimentation, despite delays and setbacks… The horrors.

{:} {:} {:} {:} {:}

The Primaviscera, I cannot see. The queen seemed to let it alone after her conquest, preferring to sit comfortably on her throne and watch all things from there. Yet, while I cannot see it, I can feel great trouble from there, and fear, a cold clawing fear, as the beating of many hands on a closed door by some unknown energies. It feels like it will sting and strangle my being to venture beyond that door. I feel that terror will tear the inner workings of my mind in ways the queen has yet to exhaust upon her own slaves.

{:} {:} {:} {:} {:}

Another private practice there was for the queen. One she designated for an instance of her – another her – to experience without foreseeable end. It was a Chandelis (a form akin to a chandelier). She had men gathered into an enormous hall, hot with red mist. All was red. The walls were indistinguishable. It seemed the hall had no boundaries.

The queen rose to a great height from the center of this hall, levitating in stillness. Her eyes gracefully closed, and she held her arms bent up above her with hands open, as though holding a great pot. Her legs transformed. Tendrils emerged, as with a creature we do not often encounter on our shores, gelatinous, soft skin, it can alter its color and form to deceive both prey and predator, having eight limbs which it contorts as the bodies of worms and serpents, and it usually scours the sea depths.

With these tendrils, the queen reached down to the hundreds of men assembled and slipped each limb into their mouths. By this, she lifted them into the air and held them hung. Their bodies seized in horror as she drained them of life. But the draining did not end, and neither did they. They remained suspended, uttering stressed moans from constant pain. Their eyes lost the will to see, and turned pale. Never did they close. The men's faces, if one could see as I do, were mangled in suffering, only able to wince and twitch. This, was the queen's meditation. Her Chandelis.

Although appearing the abstraction of a sea dweller, the queen also portrayed another, far worse creature, one rarely spoken of for fear of her great manifestation. The many cultures of Patashan share a pantheon of gods and wicked ones. By many names they are known, yet, to the Comempri, the king of demons was called, Dialeshri. It is his lesser known, yet greater feared sister I speak of – Hashara Dia.

In the book, Songs of Dialesh, Hashara's image resembles Gishona's Chandelis, many tendrils holding men in suspension, draining them of life for eternity while Dialeshri ate the women. She is said to possess women discarded by the flows of life, and the unforgiving machinations of man. Through the woman's frail mind, Hashara Dia brings all to submission. As the hand of the demon king, she gathers male and female, subjugates them, tortures them, and brings them to Dialeshri as gifts. She herself bows to her elder brother, and for her terrible deeds, he rewards her with all the male souls she desires, whilst he prepares the women for meal. It is also written that he forcefully mates with her, and she willingly, lovingly, surrenders to him. To her, Dialeshri is not only her elder brother, but also her god. It is her devotion to him which makes her so terribly dangerous.

It is also written that to speak of her, especially by a woman's mouth, invites her into that woman's house, and if she has a family, every female risks haunting, and every male risks rape and torment, while they yet live. Some women, reports say, have willingly invited her to sate their own retribution.

I do not know for certain, even now, if Hashara Dia is the embodiment of Gishona, or Gishona the embodiment of Hashara Dia. Nevertheless, I suspect the stories of Dialeshri and his sister, bear some truth, somehow. I am at the door. Behind is the answer. But the burden of knowledge far exceeds my capacity. Perhaps another can do the deed. Bless those who do.

There is more, so much more that Gishona did. So much more that she planned. But what is here inscribed will suffice, so that we all understand this threat. The rest is yours to find.

CHAPTER 23

THE PILES

CX23

It is appropriate that I address this last horror, before my thoughts are eclipsed by that great light.

There was a catacomb underground, akin to the palace depths. In this catacomb were many dead, of men and animals, bodies broken, limbs, bones, and dismembered flesh in great heaps three men high, mingled with all manner of waste. They were left to rot and their fumes to become thick and ferment with putrefaction. Large braziers rising to near the ceiling gave enough light for all to be seen just clearly enough.

Why? The queen thought it a fitting joke for men, that the living should be thrown in with the dead for a time to see themselves the way she saw them. There was no respite from the filth. Though the great piles remained more to the walls of the catacombs, the ground between them and around them was thick with mud made of waste, a special brew of all remains ground together and saturated with water. It rose to half a leg, and its consistency made walking through it a cumbersome affair. It was much too easy for one to occasionally trip and fall in.

The smell alone made men sick – enough to die. So thick was the putrid air that it amassed a visible fog. Worse still, the entire cave system was purposefully overrun with fungus, flies, worms, maggots, and all manner of budding life-forms which thrive on waste. Colonies were so extensive that the sounds of creeping, slithering, and buzzing were easily heard. The scent of men was indistinguishable from the stink, swiftly drawing the attention of any creeping thing. Men were left there for as many days as it took for them to be sufficiently diseased, malnourished, and defiled by vermin. Nevertheless, they were not allowed to die from their suffering.

The catacomb of the dead was a more unique creation, crafted by the Diamet through dark ritual.

Once released, men were presented to the queen by the Diamet, so that she could laugh herself silly at their condition, and then whip them with cords of metal, tearing off flesh with every lash. When every part of them bled, and the queen was satisfied, she took from them her essence, so they could die of their wounds and join the dead.

The method of selecting which men would suffer the catacomb, was nothing more than for the queen to choose any man whensoever she wished. Never those delivered unto Primahorica.

No more. I have no more horrors, for all that I have recorded. I have so many volumes recounting her deeds. This is an attempt to render to you, perhaps the most important observations, vulgar though they are. She is a horror, amalgams multiplied, which has no business here, yet here she is, existing beyond any available reason conjured by humanity. Nevertheless, something here drew her into existence, or else, here she would not be. But now the turning, for my thoughts are eclipsed. That great light soothes my script for finer tellings. I speak now of the arrival of the star, the flame, Theiander, of the Guthamen Isles.

CHAPTER 24

THAT GREAT LIGHT

CX24

The Hot Season had ended. The start of a new year. A frenzy was initiated. All Isscaran everywhere, were commanded to hunt and terrorize to their will's content, all males in every city and settled part of Patashan. It was left to their individual choice whether to terrorize women awaiting their turn for Primahorica, for the glory of the new woman.

It happened all at once. A single day. From the morning on. It was early, as those who slept from exhaustion stirred. Sleep, as you might imagine, did not come easily in Patashan then. It had not for a long time. The Isscaran took to men like a brood of yegal (hyenas) to a fresh carcass, pinning them with their backs to the ground, immobilizing them, and all together chewing away flesh, often from the bottom to the chest, amongst other things. They beat them and threw them about, playing and thrashing in whatever ways they chose.

Age did not matter. Though the younger a male, the more likely they were to be subjected to the art of fear. The Isscaran became as monsters in the shadows, charging through house walls or sneaking in to frighten with creeping laughter and horrid noises. And what they did to them otherwise…I was so torn. Less a fit of violence than foreplay, taunting of pleasures while boys feared for their lives at every moment, never knowing when fright would turn to feast. How long this lasted is anyone's suspicion. No child deserved such things. It was all the more twisted how the Isscaran favored boys in transition to a body they did not yet understand.

Howls and screams. Howls and screams. Howls, and screams. Everywhere. As I watched from the palace peak, my eyes viewing the all of Patashan, the queen took me from behind and carried me to her bed chambers. Without a word, she pinned me down on her bed and overwhelmed me again with so many iterations of herself at one time.

The process was different here. My body took the full brunt of her passions, yet I was somewhere else, on a plain of sand, resting on my knees in its softness, across from that woman of light who sat as I did, our hands folded in peace. In that space, we spoke, with the sun's gift of light all around us, soft and soothing. I asked her, "How much longer?"

She smiled and said, "No more waiting."

I asked, "By what miracle comes our peace?"

She said, "By light in you, the answer lives. By light you see the answer gives. By light for all, the answer thrives."

I asked, "Are there others like you?"

She said, "Many. They are here, waiting."

I said, "I understand."

I awakened to a startled face, the first time I saw that in her. Eyes wide with a shock of disgust and sadness. I betrayed her somehow. They all looked at me this way. I looked at my skin, and it again glowed. I saw her hand up to her chin, and the seared flesh on her arm. It happened. And she was far too shocked to remove herself.

But there was no time for her to process what she felt, for then, a blast. Energy thrust her back, and all her iterations inside her, from every part of the continent. Light flooded her chambers. I rose to fully invite it within myself, and formed with it, new garments.

All across Patashan, there was a sudden shift. Isscaran awakened as out of death, realizing themselves in the act of squeezing their victims in their hands, chewing flesh, or on the hunt, and were horrified. Their own hands offended them, frightened them. Many screamed as by nightmare's terror, not recognizing who they were, where or why. Some beheld their victims suffering and wept, desperately scrambling to close wounds. They held young men in their arms, pressed tight to their bodies, begging forgiveness only by tears and wailing. They were humans again.

And the people, were suddenly drained of fear, their minds quieted to serenity, free from the buzzing, clawing and roaring of horrors in their minds, their eyes seeing in bright volumes of love manifested. Those whose bodies were torn apart, fully mended themselves in an instant, to better than prior to their torture. There was no anger toward their captors, no vengeful intent against their assailants. No wicked thing existed in those moments. They only saw and felt beings who loved them. Beings whom they also loved.

The queen coughed and heaved. Her eyes seemed anxious to eject from their sockets. Refusing to give in, she struggled to her feet, growling, ;; *No!* ;; and with a thrust of her hands, forced a wave of dark energy to flood the continent, undoing the light that was. Nearly all things returned to what they were, the Isscaran plunged into worse monstrosity than before, more wild, more ravenous, more enraged. Most people returned also to their state of fear and terror. However, some were a little less so than before, and began to fight back. I maintained my new garments.

Here is where it could be clearly seen how much influence the queen had over Patashan. So much of her strength had grown in subtlety, beginning with the Isscaran, when she fed her power to the first to partake of her sacrament. Then more forcefully in the battle of Balashah, in Issacre when she initiated the time of sacrifice, of testing, of Primahorica, and all that came after and throughout. Her power was truly great, having multiplied in all those she blessed and tormented, and the bounty having returned to her.

A few moments later, just as the queen held her grimacing head high with pride, the light rebounded even stronger. The queen fell back, nearly paralyzed with frail bones and burning skin. A childish wine was heard from her, and her voice trembled as her body convulsed.

I left her to again stand at the edge of the palace peak and look out to all things. Slaves were slaves no longer. Those whose minds were broken by her script now walked fearlessly. Many the Isscaran felt their minds strained by the push and pull, and turned to the palace begging the queen to stop. There were some who resisted the light, choosing in that moment of clarity to maintain the power they knew, and the pain that came with it. Still, they were powerless against those once their victims. Yet, where they found their footing in pain, other Isscaran found their relief, completely letting go their inner torment.

Again, the queen struggled to rise. More difficult this time. Again, she pushed and forced her darkness, and again monstrosity returned, though now with firm resistance on both sides. Isscaran resisted Isscaran, defending their former captives, some of whom stood with them, more empowered by that great light. Those who remained fearful, now found saviors in every corner where darkness seemed to prevail. I beheld those slaves most broken ascend the steps in battalions as though trained soldiers, passing me by with barely a look my way. The queen was soon to be confronted.

But then as they smashed the doors in, the light returned three-fold and silenced all Patashan. Isscaran on the attack were instantly withheld from their victims, blocked off by an invisible, ethereal boundary, blurring their sight as they pulled away. They reached with all their anger, swiped forward with all their strength, but all was silence and nothingness. It was as though they were alone – sequestered in their own space. All citizens of Patashan walked free, no fear of anything at all, and able to go on with their lives.

The queen was stricken petrified and deaf, huddled in a corner of her chambers, trembling and catatonic. The men who broke in beheld her mercifully, with kind expressions. They lifted her gently into her bed and covered her body in blankets.

The great light persisted in this way for months. The queen eventually fought herself back to strength in her body, able to move about as before, though with a limp and a piercing pain in her gut, which she also resisted. She attempted to assert control once again, but nothing came of it. No energy left to dispatch. Even those Isscaran still loyal to her, found themselves just as fruitless, able to move about, fully in control of their faculties, except in doing harm – the one thing they were groomed to do.

Queen Gishona could not command anything. The Isscaran, if given order to dominate or inflict trauma, could not obey for all their willpower. She looked to me, angry, again betrayed by my own light, by my garments, void of her design, by my youth, finer than her ceasefire upon the natural deterioration of time. For all her desire, she could not even scream in anger. Tears dripped from pools in her eyes instead, and she returned to her chambers.

She slowly deteriorated to dormancy, sometimes pacing about her room lost in idle wonder. Eventually, she laid herself in bed and stopped altogether. The only sign of activity was the wideness of her eyes, never blinking and never moving. I stood in front of her once. She was turned on her right shoulder, facing her left, frozen. I stared into her eyes, my light glowing, and yet, I was nothing to her. But as I walked away, in my thoughts I heard her call me by my name, my full name, Achmed Al Hadid. She had never addressed me this way. Desperation, ran its course.

CHAPTER 25

THEIANDER

I endured these months in peace, able to have friends and become part of a community. I freely left the palace after so many years dedicated to the queen's purpose. There was goodness everywhere. All the Isscaran loyal to the empire could do was grimace upon my passing by, and fall bitter at the sight of their once sisters welcoming me with warmth of greetings, tight embracing, and gratitude.

It was on the last day of the seventh month that we all felt a pulse pass through the earth beneath us and above. I remained close to Her Fury, in my exploration of Issacre, ever watching her condition. I had never seen her like that before; such a prolonged moment of powerlessness.

The sound of singing was heard in the air, millions upon millions of voices humming as one. The song was of joy – a gentle, peaceful, wonderous joy. At times, it flowed like waves of water to a shoreline, alternating between chords of harmony complementing the core melody, and Gishona's former slaves blissfully swam right into it, matching their voices to the sound. The queen was compelled to know what this was. Though it pained her to stand, she forced herself as she did all things, and went to wait on the palace steps. She would not go any further, as it was now her right to see all things from above, and for all things to come to her from below.

She stood for a long stretch of time waiting, stoic, with eyes fixed on the horizon, until beyond the gates of the palace district, she saw a sea of golden light, glistening as the evening sun on the waters. When at last the gates opened, the golden sea poured in, as if from a world unknown to us, where our gods are said to glimpse the Eternal Orbis – Banshamat.

The queen's skin boiled and stung for a few seconds when light rays met her body. Her skin remained irritated from then on.

The singing accumulated form and volume as the procession of light drew near the palace steps, inciting the queen's skin to shiver with rage. In passing, people gathered at their wings, stood by and let their voices become song.

The Isscaran who did not take part, attempted spite with everything in their being, but were absent the energy to act on their feelings. Some receded within themselves, neutralized, stalemated, finding no reason to hate. Indeed, they searched for motive to force their way, as to coerce a horse to motion, and that horse refuse to move, no matter their effort. Though, it was hard for them to hide the insult they felt as they witnessed their sisters passing by, untethered from the bond they all forged.

A short way from the palace steps, the procession ceased, and the song gracefully concluded. So near, the light to the queen burned as the sun to her subjects in the hot season. The fight she mustered was as clear as the hardened muscles in her face, her glaring eyes, and her solid grip on her stomach. She began a slow descent, measuring every step, each one a little more painful than the last. At midway, she nearly collapsed, tears running over weeping pores. Sweat made her shine in the sun. She gritted her teeth, fighting. But what exactly?

It was at the last step that she collapsed on one knee, catching herself with her left hand, whilst her right remained fused to her stomach. Her breathing was fraught with fret, making known to the ears her struggle. After a moment, she stood, fighting the compulsion to step forward. Something inside compelled her. She felt herself moving despite her resistance.

Growls and grunts forced themselves through clenched teeth, grinding shut. Her body thrust itself forth, pushing her to the ground before a man and a woman standing beside one another in front of the crowd. For a moment, she could not move except to tremble and catch her breath with heavy heaves. The man and woman looked at each other with firm yet placid stares, absent of judgment, then looked again at the queen.

Furious with impatience, the queen looked up to the pair, then to the left and right of them, brought to outrage and disgust at the sight of her Isscaran staring back at her, saturated by light and void of her imprint. She roared and lunged upward at the man and woman. At this instant, as if by foresight, their hands moved in concert, blocking her arms low with their inner hands, and reaching her head with their outer hands to touch the queen's third eye by their thumbs together. Light concentrated and she awakened.

In an instant, the queen was surrounded by bright light of many colors. She stood enamored by the sight, looking about with new eyes and a child's glare of wonder and amazement. For the first time, she was unable to process the darkness she loved, looking upon herself as though a stranger in her own body. She muttered muffled speech of incoherent words in broken patterns. Her eyes fluttered as she struggled to process these strange surroundings.

There was a portion of golden light before her like a wall, and out of it stepped the form of a man, walking toward her. With each step, his light melted away to reveal the man, youthful, skin a golden hue as the sands of our shores on a slender yet fortified physique, as one whose body knew the waters, rich black hair, pulled to the left side in thin, braided strands the length of the sternum, decorated with beads. His only garment was a pair of pants, beige in color, whose material flowed without wrinkle, and shoes of crystal which bent as would leather. Despite appearing no older than twenty years, in his face was an aged calm with a leisurely smile, as one who had lived longer than me, for whom all human yearnings were satisfied by uncontested understanding.

"Many pleasures to you. I am Theiander," he said first.

The rest, I leave to another. Gishona's path to Shivana. The telling of Theiander's story is better suited for one still attuned to the bindings of the Red Queen. Perhaps someone who knew her in a way that I could not. Here is where my memory of their words, one to another, dissolves. Here is where my record of her horrors end. For all my well-being, you see, the burden had finally expired. My body, my mind, had no more capacity to hold on, and no more need to. It was done, and so was I.

It was only moments after Theiander's arrival and introduction that I was released from the queen's service, by her own mouth. Away, she said to me.

;; Away Achmed Al Hadid. Fair you to fairer shores than to wade the waters which flow from me and have swaddled you to sink. Though with all I sought to swallow you, you would not descend. You would not digest. Away with you. No more Hepatsu. Away. For finer light would see me through a loveless loss and darker toss. Where now will I rest that you are gone? Where now am I? Away. ;;

By her blessing, I let go. Let go a link which never was, except in imitation. No more the mask of Hepatsu. No more a king. Erushad must now grow without me. Yes, in present I speak of Eru. It must always grow without me.

As I walked away, I looked to no one and I saw nothing, save my own path forward, alight with brilliance of love. Peace forever. I walked away, letting fall the pains of horrors. Only the book in my hand. Her book. Her story, in part. Forget I did, for a time, to let my mind soften, my soul rest. Then to pick up memory again so I could finish what I began in writ.

CHAPTER 26

FINAL REMARKS

With these assorted passages, I conclude my conjecture. My words here are last thoughts and scattered observations before I tell you what I see.

& & &

A thought I pose to you. It is not the exposure to horrors which enlightened me, but clinging to enlightenment through it all. For while the struggle to survive may strengthen some, that strength is forced by necessity. I found my strength by journeying inward, and allowing that great light within to express my path through all the darkness which sought to dim that light. It may seem a lofty thing, but the way of peace also gives power to those who keep it. To this end, we must be willing to see ourselves for all the good that we are and can be, never belittling what we have, even if it seems inadequate to the forces arrayed against us.

& & &

I understand why some might choose to idolize this man, Theiander, but, if idolization were a sensible thing, then he would return the favor. He is a man, with a home, a people, a land of wealth all-fulfilling, and an inner hearth of love, abundant and unchanging. This man came so that we could have the same. Perhaps, when his story is told in full, you will understand.

& & &

The Comempri kings, those who survived, never did fully recover from their humiliation, before Theiander. With all the pleasures they experienced, they could not deny the sight of horrors all around them. Each in his own way, looked upon the pains of their world and realized there was nothing left but pain. They had given all to be kings of nothing, despite the truth of Gishona's promises.

They were safe from danger, but not from trauma. And so, they had only to surrender themselves to the queen's pleasure, to drown out the noise, the aches in their souls, and the frailty of their minds, gaining in fragility, as their queen gained in dominance. She promised them, every night. They needed all day and night. They begged for it, debased themselves to have more, until only she existed in them. Their minds were left derelict by overwhelming stimuli, such as what she attempted with me.

When the great light of Theiander graced the continent, the kings had their opportunity to choose a new way. Whether or not they did, is beyond me to say.

    &   &   &

What of the children of Jivaldi and Farasha Hamheti? The handmaidens of Farasha were swift and foreseeing. Bearing the Hamheti sons yet remaining in Patashan far out to sea. As the elders know the coming of the storm, so did they know the turning of unfamiliar troubles inbound by she who sundered their house. My light tells me that they found their own source within themselves, and now wander the world with the ancients. Shivana may attempt to find them, but the light hides them, as the sun blinds the eyes. The house first troubled by a jealous queen was spared the horrors to come. To what end? We will see.

    &   &   &

When I left Gishona, I took only one book, one mostly absent of words, as all the memory of what was written in every volume is in my mind, exactly as it was written. And as for Theiander, I did ask him by thought and spirit, how it was he arrived seven years after his summoning? He by thought and spirit answered me this,

"My people were assaulted by the mere whisper of the Red Queen's energy, seven years past. Assault, a word we did not know until now. Her spirit broke on our shores with the tide, like a storm come to land from the open seas. We did not know pain, and so it nearly destroyed us. We did not have words for destruction until now. I watched my brothers, sisters, friends, sink to the water's depths, after violent darkness overwhelmed their inner light. We knew neither violence nor darkness, save the beautiful night.

We wept. We did not know weeping. We feared. We did not know fear. We were angry. We did not know anger. But we had our way, our living way. Instead of break, we gathered from all over the isles to our Yevan tree, that which freely gives the energy I share, and we together processed this foreign, violent way for seven years.

So long a time was required, as we all had to share in concentration, collecting our energies as one being, so we did not process this one's violence too quickly, and so that no one person took on too much. This violence is entangled and eating itself always. As the threads of our tapestries, we had to untangle every delicate thread, each one poison to us all, and fashion a language by which we could read this foreign way. Words we did not know before, we know now. Feelings we did not need to feel before, we feel now.

We, the gathering, hundreds of thousands, moved in concert. The universe met us from the sky to balance our process. For every word materialized, for every thread untangled and threaded again, for every feeling given sound and meaning, each was moved into place, as with the game board, each piece carefully set, until the whole board is filled — a beautiful tapestry reflecting all of existence. Wheels within wheels, every shape and shade, and all symmetry.

The darkness was kept outside by careful hands and filtered slowly into each inner level, so it would not overwhelm. We shifted from the base to the peak of our great tapestry, until the last word came to me, and I shifted to the top. My word was, Nabatuum – obscura, the unfathomed obscurity. Upon the threading of this word, the universe asked my name. I said, Theiander, and all spoke my name thrine (thrice) in unison, my people and the council of the universe. On this, I was elected. Had another shifted to the peak, he or she would have been elected. A balance of mass and fine-tuned sound. Had we gone any faster or slower, had we severed our patient flow, there would come no help for any of you, from the Guthamen Isles. Now we know the ways of our eternal ancestors, as they thread our tapestry always, so we are not overwhelmed."

I understand. I understood. I am forever grateful for the Guthamen and for what we by them have learned.

& & &

I did eventually meet a woman with whom I flourished in love. She was every bit the goddess Gishona thought herself to be. Her love for me was without measure. Kind where the Red Queen was cruel, a healing light in contrast of every way Gishona burgeoned in darkness, and she rewrote the memories of abuses laid upon my mind and body by Her Fury. The treatment of the Red Queen toward me, though ever present, is nevertheless a series of fragmented forms having no value or prominence to my being, other than record. All sense of value and prominence is now mantled gracefully by my lover, Emansca. And it is as though we have been together for all time.

CHAPTER 27

WHAT I SEE

CX27

What I see with my eyes, my mind remembers as though always present, and the more I remember, the more I can predict and visualize what is to come.

What I see now, with all that I have recounted to you, is what follows.

Limited to her entrapment below, Shivana relies on her influence spread throughout the surface world. She still has the Isscaran, now more indebted and devoted to her than before. Their pain is entwined with her own, and they are her last and foremost defense, no matter who or what others she employs.

She has designs. All she did in Patashan was the beginning. Read you the broken map of that once continent. In it, is her sacred script, her vision of an entire world. She will rewrite her story to paint herself the image of divine ascension. The arrival of Theiander will forever be affixed to her mind, an event she cannot bring herself to dominate. She may instead choose to venerate.

He is ever the stone she cannot reach, buried deep inside the earth. The new jewel to be laced around her neck, if she could claim it. Until such an opportunity presents itself, she will claim other stones, rough, needing to be polished, and attempt to make them worthy enough to be the jewel, if not the jewel itself. She is impatient always, yet patient. Trusting no one. Many fingers reaching far to enforce control of what is rendered vulnerable to her. She gives power to all her many subjects, limiting their range so that, should they fail, her energy returns to her, all their acquired knowledge intact, and none of their failures.

Shivana's many fragments of mind are divided, scattered throughout the earth, with a small collective struggling to remain adhered to her. She is cracked, shattered shards mortared together, and risks diaspora of all her disparate parts. Moreso, she was likely burned by Theiander's light, by her own impatience I imagine, or by her desire to dominate. It may have been similar to being burned by me when I woke from my trance. I do not know what that would do to her at such high concentrations, however, I see her unable to process that light, one way or another. The light may be what fractures, as any mind which cannot comprehend it.

Existing in her vulnerable yet venomous state, she will seek territory to claim, as she did in Patashan, both of land and living ones. Monsters are inevitable. She must fulfill her experiments. Sisterhoods are inevitable. She will still attempt to redefine the woman. Dark ritual and twisting of the known world are inevitable. She endeavors to insert herself into all things, whatsoever she can, and grow her power over time. She also seeks to absorb any powerful being which may oppose or obstruct her intent. Centralized power as always.

There is great brilliance in her. Great brilliance. The shadow of a light she once proudly mantled. Go to the abandoned city of Abnashila to see her wonders. It is located just southwest of Issacre itself, linked by a great road one hundred lexims wide and half a mile long. Many walls surround it, a combined structure looming over the inner cities, taller than the palace. She wanted to be able to see it from her throne.

Keep watch for the children of Gishona, before she became Shivana, those who scattered throughout the world. They are as whirlwinds of water out in the open seas, drawing energies into themselves unbeknownst to most. Though trained to mantle their mother's ways, they are yet agents of obscure variable. Their chosen paths are yet to be determined. I see that they may test every land to one end or another. Hopefully, balance is the result.

The Red Queen tortured and tormented hundreds of millions of people in her time, and slew millions more. I see that even after Theiander, so many remain in their torment, choosing the desolation of Her Fury, or unable to find their way to their inner light, even with Theiander's aid. Millions of Mahakra, faithful covens and subjugated servants. Many more are scorned to ambivalence after all things, disillusioned by the struggle between the red rage and that great light, ultimately electing to abide without either of them. Many still, though fewer, have joined to their inner light and go their own way. Trophies which the Red Queen cannot reclaim.

The known world might remain contested ground for many years. I see much confusion, debate, the twisting of powers, and the longing to improve on past failures, with many disparate ideals forced to prominence. I do see a coalition of powers – a reimagined Comempri. There are many possibilities for what they might create. Though their influence will sway between malevolence and beneficence, according to what they deem most beneficial to their will.

Darkness, as any sickness does, will lie and fester in the periphery of the earth, whilst the known world reshapes itself. Traversal of the waters between will prove difficult. Storms trouble the seas.

What of our ancients? Seek them out. We all know them, deep inside us. They are distant, yet nearer to us than those we are born to. I see them, always a great benefit. Though some embody great tragedy, and by their own scars, score the earth for better and worse.

Restore connection to the guides hidden in the earth. I see their scattering and descent. The longing to reconnect and aid us in our light paths never ebbs. Soldiering men will struggle to understand these great spirits. A gentler touch is required. And so they will hide as gems in aged soil until the gentle find them, ready to receive. Where and when they are most needed, is where and when they are most available.

The rest, I leave you to discover. Study the map of Shivana's doings in Patashan, here rendered plain for your eyes. What I write to you, I do so with awareness of interception, that my words might be seen by the unintended. As such, I present here things which are known, and things which can be perceived by many. The bounty is yours to find, dear reader. There is something deeper. Find it.

And fear not for me. I am beyond the reach of all ill will.

I understand the detail of these passages may be found greatly cumbersome. That encumbrance is its own strand of truth. The world needs to know about Shivana, the Void Mother, the Red Queen. We must know. Be not mistaken; it is not for fear, but preparation and understanding. I say again, she is a horror, amalgams multiplied, which has no business here, yet here she is, existing beyond any available reason conjured by humanity.

Nevertheless, something here drew her into existence on this world, or else, here she would not be. Find it. What that is; find it. We must know. We must know how she thinks, what she feels, how she operates. We must know her design, the thoughts she keeps, the thoughts she shares, and the power she withholds or spares. We must know how she behaves, how she hides, how she hoards, how she fights, how her appendages move throughout the world. We must know what vast and much faceted horrors are prepared for us, should she take hold of the earth. We must know her madness, the suffering we could endure, and the plight of those who suffer by her now. She will not cease if she is allowed what she desires. She does not know how. She lacks as much control of herself as she casts upon the world. We must know. The whole earth must know. As much of it can know.

And in this, what she always desired is accomplished...to be remembered.

One last observation I have for you. There is something to be found in her earliest relations with the three young men. The first young man left her after a short while, when he realized she was far too much trouble for his comforts. The second, the brawler, mysteriously died after spending a more substantial amount of time with her, enough for her to have decided she loved him. The third, she feared to lose after experiencing a taste of genuine love in one day, and killed him by the works of her own hands, shortly thereafter.

Bear this in mind. One to flee before too long, one to die – it seems – beyond her control, and one to die by her hands. Her mother died bearing her here this world – the closest she has ever been to anyone.